Springtime in Paris

Lilita Correia

Writers Club Press
San Jose New York Lincoln Shanghai

Published by Writers Club Press
an imprint of iUniverse.com, Inc.

For information address:
iUniverse.com, Inc.
620 North 48th Street
Suite 201
Lincoln, NE 68504-3467
www.iuniverse.com

ISBN: 0-595-00775-9

Printed in the United States of America

One

What Emily wanted was spring. It was a dark cloudy afternoon and it was one of those days when everyone seemed to be depressed about something. When the depression hit, Emily chose to read a romantic novel, mainly because there wasn't much else she could do. She let her imagination run away with her to a romantic place.

But not this time. She was so amazed and still not quite ready to believe it. She was really going on a trip! She had slept a lot longer that morning, as her spirits were up and she had felt so relaxed.

Now though, she had finished packing her red Samsonite. She was anxious for her first trip abroad. But there were still a few hours before departure.

Emily came down to the living room, where her older sister and her son were watching television. Meanwhile, her mother was in the kitchen preparing lunch for all of them. Emily sat down on the sofa, close to her sister.

Edite had arrived a week earlier to spend three weeks with her parents and sister. But Emily's trip was already planned. She didn't want to cancel. After all this was the first voyage without her parents.

Emily played with little John and his Lego set. All children like to construct with those blocks.

When Emily's mother had lunch ready, she came down to the living room, to ask her two daughters to come up to for lunch.

"Emily…Edite…The lunch is ready."

"Mamma…we will go up in a minute."

"I will take John up for his lunch."

"Thanks mamma." Edite politely thanked her mother. She loved the leisure of doing absolutely nothing or at least the minimum. The two sisters were talking about anything and everything; it had been along time since they had seen each other. Their mother called them again.

"Come on you two the food is getting cold."

"All right, mamma. We are coming." The two sisters walked up to the kitchen. John was eating his lunch slowly. Emily sat down close by the widow, while her sister sat on the opposite side. Her mother set the food platter on the table.

They all had a pleasant and relaxing lunch. The only person missing at the table was their father. He was working at his office, where he was running a business.

The rest of the afternoon passed fairly quickly. Then it was time to get ready to leave for the airport. Her father arrived later.

It took her father twenty minutes to arrive at the airport. It took longer to find a free parking space. It was one of the busiest seasons of the year. There were a lot of happy travelers going on spring break.

Emily stepped out quickly from the elevator at the departure floor. She walked towards the KLM airlines counter. There were already a line, where the recognized a few of her classmates. But it didn't take long for her to check in. Meanwhile, her family was waiting for her. Emily was very excited about going on the trip. She was travelling with her class-mates from her Art Club and of course, there were two of her teachers coming along. They were both art teachers, but teaching different grades. They were both outstanding teachers and very outgoing. Everyone liked them and both enjoy their students.

"I am ready, we could go, to the lounge for something to drink." Emily held the hand of her nephew, and the rest of the family came along. There were still times until boarding.

They walked in to the self -serve cafeteria and looked at what they had. Then everyone went to find a table and sat down, while Emily and her father went to pick up what they had chosen.

"Well, Emily how are you feeling?" Mr. Antonio asked his daughter, knowing it very well that she was a bit nervous. But at the same time he knew it that his daughter was happy. He had said yes although her mother was very apprehensive of letting her go.

"I am a bit nervous and at the same time looking forward to it."

Minutes later, there were two trays with soft drinks, three cups of coffee and two chocolate donuts.

Mr. Antonio paid at the cashier and Emily was the first one to set the tray down.

They sat there drinking their coffee. Meanwhile, John was enjoying his chocolate donut.

Emily glanced at her watch and saw it was the time for her to be boarding. Then she said to everyone at table.

"Well…that it is. It is time to be leaving."

She got up and picked her up handbag and coat everyone did the same. They all walked by her side until they couldn't go any further. She embraced her sister and bent down to kiss her nephew. Then he said to her, "Bye auntie Emily."

"Good-bye John." She embraced him tenderly.

Then she embraced her parents. Then she went through the airport security and then turned around waved back to them. Her parents waved back to her too and she stood there for a moment. Then she went walking on the corridor until she found the right departure area. She right away recognized some of her fellow passengers.

Emily walked in and an airline employee handed her the boarding pass. Then she sat down on the black leather sofa. She waited as a lot of thoughts came on her mind. After just a few minutes there were a lot of passengers waiting and some were impatient.

Emily realized it was best to put away her passport. She needed only the boarding pass. Afterwards there was nothing to worry about. She sat there content. Suddenly someone sat beside her.

"Hi…Emily."

"Hello Sarah are you excited?" She found out that it was Sarah's first flight and she was a bit uneasy. But Emily assured her it would be all right.

"I am feeling better since we will be sitting beside each other."

"They should be calling us soon."

Meanwhile Emily got up and she stepped inside the ladies room. Moments after being inside she heard a female voice announcing the flight number 204 to Amsterdam was boarding. Immediately Emily finished brushing her hair then she came out. A few fellow passengers were walking through the arcade, which lead them to the boarding entrance.

Emily seat number was towards the back. Minutes later she was sitting down on the outside seat. Sarah sat by Elizabeth as the three of them became friends. The two other girls were much closer to each other age. Emily was much older than the two.

After a while all the passengers were all sitting down. Then the captain spoke.

"Ladies and Gentlemen we will be taking off shortly." The captain was waiting for the go ahead from the tower. But minutes later the captain was taking off. They were on their way to a fun week to Paris.

But their arrival at their final destination would take longer because they were going via Amsterdam. Afterwards they would be taking the charter bus to Paris.

After being in the air for a while the flight attendants began serving drinks while they heated up the dinner trays.

Meanwhile Emily spoke to their friends both seemed to be very cheerful.

"Emily how did you end up coming?" Elizabeth asked her because she had to press her parents.

She really wanted to go. Emily told her the same story, which her mother didn't want her to come. But after a while she said yes.

"Elizabeth it wasn't easy. But we all are here." They all were happy they would be joining each other company.

"Oh! Well. Let's enjoy our dinner." Sarah said. Knowing very well they wouldn't eat much.

"Right." Emily said with a very enthusiastic answer.

Finally all the dinner trays were taken away. Then Emily tried to close her eyes for a little bit. She was tired from a long day. After all it was getting late it had been a few hours in flight.

As soon as Emily thought she was going to doze off she was quick awakened by a nuisance from the back of the plane. There was a lot of movement back and forth.

A few of the older boys were drinking a lot of beers and at one point two of them really got sick from drinking so much alcohol.

Emily wasn't used to seeing that kind of behavior. After all she was trying to sleep and it annoyed her. The whole night was an excess of movement at the back of the plane.

Emily some how managed to close her eyes for a quiet moment. Her exhaustion began to show and she felt it. She was so tired and that was just the beginning.

Later on the time seemed to pass quickly as then she noticed the breaking in the daylight. A few passengers were pulling the window shades. The sun was just beginning to rise which it was an exquisite site and for a moment the sign of fasten seat belts came on. There were a few moments of turbulence but it subsided. The sign was turned off and the flight attendants began serve a warm breakfast. By then everyone seemed to be very hungry. Emily ate the warm croissants, and by then it tasted so good with a cup of coffee. From that point on the time went quickly.

Finally the plane touched down at Schirphol Airport. It was a very early hour in the morning at that time the airport was really empty.

Emily walked along the vast empty corridor with her fellow passengers. After walking the long empty corridors for a little while she got to the officials. One big line began forming they all were anxious to move along. But first they had to go through the Dutch officials.

Emily waited for her turn. When it came to her return the male official looked at her and asked a lot of questions.

But she answered all of them. At that point the official stamped her passport.

She wondered about so many questions. It was so easy to see right away because there was no other flight. Emily follows the others to the baggage area where she didn't have to wait too long. She saw her red Samsonite coming on the conveyor belt.

Quickly she walked outside as everyone was already there. All of them waited outside for their charter bus to arrive. She felt the cool breeze on her face. There were signs of spring all around as the tulips were blooming.

Meanwhile Emily walked towards Sarah and Elizabeth and asked one of them to take a photo of her. She stood there with Sarah while Elizabeth took her photo.

Elizabeth had short reddish hair and also had glasses. She was taller than Sarah who had long blond hair and was also friendly. After waiting a long while the charter bus arrived. Immediately the driver began loading into the bus their suitcases. Meanwhile they stepped inside and sat down. Emily sat by the window side on the center of the bus. She relaxs as it was a long drive from Amsterdam to Paris.

The two teachers from her high school were very likeable all around. They had a very easy personality. They both were friendly toward the students and they in return liked them. Mrs. King had a Ph.D. in art and as she taught at the school and on her spare time she painted. The other teacher was younger and she had been teaching at that high school for a shorter period of time. She was from European background. Miss Stella helped if someone needed her.

It was the first time that high school had organized a large excursion like that one. The others trips had always been small scale.

The driver loaded all the baggage into the trunk of the bus. It was a matter of minutes before the driver began to drive away from the airport towards the highway. The morning seemed to pass quickly and at the same time it got warmer.

The scenery was quite different as the driver passed by the countryside where they were able to see the famous windmills.

The driver went faster somehow; Emily was by then getting really sleepy. The time was different. She closed her eyes for a moment and lay her head back. She fell asleep. It seemed like she slept for a few days but in reality only for a few hours. The driver stopped for lunch so his passengers could take some fresh air and at the same time have a bite to eat at the restaurant.

They had to walk through the tunnel to go across the other side where the restaurant was.

The two stepped out of the bus. Quickly they walked across and went to the restaurant then went in. It was very busy, as there was a line up for the exchanged currency. They both had to exchange some so they could have also something to eat.

The lunch had to be served quickly, so they sat down in one of the round tables with a group.

Afterwards they all walked back through the tunnel back to bus. Minutes later all were sitting down before the driver drove away. He checked the list to make sure all his passengers were there.

Moments later the driver drove away as he still had to go through two countries. But they didn't have to get out, just sign their names on a paper.

It was nice scenery but for so many hours travelling sitting down it was exhausting.

They passed through the beautiful city of Brussels, then as driver crossed Belgium then towards to France.

Emily fell asleep again.

Two

Finally they arrived in Paris. It was early evening as the whole group was exhausted .and all wanted to go straight to their rooms at the hotel.

But as they were in the city somehow the driver turned into a wrong narrow street in which it was a bit difficult to go through. It took the driver a long while before he could go out from that mess.

With the help of a local Frenchman he finally was able to move.

It was seven o'clock on the evening when the driver stopped at the entrance of the Penta Paris Hotel.

The hotel was located on the outskirts of Paris.

Emily and the rest of the group stepped out of the bus. They walked inside to the lobby. Meanwhile the driver took all of the baggage. Before they all got settle in, there was a lot of information to be heard. They all had to be assigned to their rooms.

An hour later Emily held her booklet of coupons. She picked her baggage and walked towards the elevator she pushed the up button. She was waiting when the other two girls to approached the elevator.

They walked around the long corridor. They saw their room number 305. It was then that Emily recognized that Sarah and Elizabeth were her roommates. Emily opened the door as all of them walked in. The room had two twin beds and a divan. The bathroom was small and just beside the entrance and on the other side was the closet and a counter with an electric kettle and a basket with a continental breakfast for three.

Emily put down her red Samsonite inside the closet. Sarah and Elizabeth looked around and they were hungry and wanted to eat something"Emily you sleep over there in one of those beds."

Elizabeth suggested politely, responded. "I will sleep on the divan." Emily said, as she tried always to be kind to the others. Sometimes she sacrificed so someone else would be more comfortable.

"You are sure Emily?" Sarah questioned her, as she was surprised at Emily's answer.

"Yes I am sure it is all right. Thanks for the suggestion."

Elizabeth decides on the bed, from the window side while her friend Sarah took the other side.

"I am going to unpacked before going down to eat something light." Emily told her new friend as she took out her nightgown and robe. After a while they went down to the restaurant.

When they got to the restaurant a lot of the group were eating.

They sat down and Emily decided to share her coupon with her two new friends. Emily browsed the menu. She understood what she read. But her friends hardly comprehended.

"Emily…do you mind translating some of the menu to us please?"

Elizabeth spoke to her as she was much more outgoing than Sarah, Emily gladly said yes to both of them.

"Yes Elizabeth…any type of sandwich? Maybe a ham and cheese there are other different type of sandwiches."

Emily browsed through the menu she chose a ham sandwich and chicken soup. She finished her dinner and walked out the restaurant. She was exhausted from along trip so many hours without sleeping. She was passing through the lobby and there was Mrs. King briefing a few of the group.

"Emily…come closer and listen."

Moments later the two other girls appear on the lobby as they seen Mrs. King speaking and they walked towards her.

"Sarah…Elizabeth are you two girls settled down yet?"

Mrs. King spoke and she had a few papers on her hand. Meanwhile everyone was approaching as they were coming out from the restaurant and the group around Mrs. King became larger.

"I have here tomorrow's itinerary. After breakfast we will be meeting here on the lobby and our first tour will be the city tour. Everyone must be here at ten o'clock."

Everyone agreed and they nodded. Minutes later, Mrs. King told them they could leave. The group spread away as each went their separate ways.

Emily walked back to the elevator she pushed the up button and waited as the other two of them came along too. Later she was opening the door. Emily got ready to go bed. But she had a few things to get done first which was to take out the clothes for the morning. Afterwards she called the operator for their awake up call.

"Are you two ready to go to sleep?"

Emily then turned the lights off as she quickly was in bed under the white sheets. She was so exhausted from not sleeping the night before and from all day travelling sitting down on the bus and which had been a tiresome journey. But she didn't seem to fall asleep. She lay awakened from all the city traffic noises. The first night was very hard for her as she was trying to sleep.

Then Monday morning came Emily was awake earlier than unusual. She had turned and turned all night. She made up her mind to get up

Since she wasn't going to sleep any longer. She got up and went to the bathroom. Elizabeth and Sarah were still sleeping.

Emily brushed her teeth then went to the bathtub where she took a shower. She felt better and awake for at least for the moment. She was ready to go sightseeing. Her spirits were up she stepped out from the bathroom. Moments later the telephone rang. It was a wakeup call.Emily picked the receiver up and then answered…

"Oui."

"Bonjour Mademoiselle."

"Merci." Emily thanked the operator.

She put the receiver down and then finished getting dressed. Afterwards she prepared her own breakfast. Soon the water was boiling she poured into a cup with an instant coffee. Then she brought the cup of coffee and the plate with two croissants and butter. She sat down on her divan and put the cup and the rest on the coffee table. She was starting to have breakfast. She remembered that Elizabeth and Sarah was still sleeping she had to awake them up.

"Good morning Elizabeth…Sarah. It is time to get up."

But as Emily had to get up a few times before they were actually up from their beds.

"It is a quarter to eight." She told them as they were still sitting down. Meanwhile Emily was having her breakfast. She slowly sipped her coffee. There was a lot time since she was ready. But for the other two they were just getting up since they had to share the bathroom and have breakfast.

After a while Emily took her red Samsonite and put everything inside and then left it inside the closet. Somehow the time passed quickly as she went down to meet Mrs. King at the lobby at the lobby.

She was the one who arrived earlier. After a long while everyone were all there.

Mrs. King began to speak to the group…

"Listen all of you. We will be leaving on the city tour around ten minutes from now. Then we will be stopping for lunch. Then we will come back to the hotel around four o'clock."

It was a wonderful spring morning, bright and sunny but on the cool side. Everyone was ready and they went into the hotels shuttle bus for a quick trip to the Tour of the city.. By ten thirty the whole group were inside of a double deck bus.

Emily sat by the window at the second deck she plugged the earphones so she could hear the English version. She had on her hand a small handy camera.

The driver spoke to the passengers…

"Good morning ladies and gentlemen we will be moving soon. Welcome to Paris Vision Tours.

We hope you all enjoy Paris merci."

Everyone was looking forward, to see the city after all, this was Paris.

Emily she was more excited than she had ever been. For her it was her first trip on her own. Although she was on her late teens but she lived a very sheltered life. There wasn't much socializing she attended school and afterwards she always went home.

But as she was in Paris a wonderful city and romance everywhere. Who knows, anything could be possible.

A female voice spoke softly in French as she explained each place passing through. There was so much history.

Emily was sitting besides an older woman in her thirties. At first there was no communication as time went through the other woman spoke to her…

"Is this your first trip to Paris?"

The other woman smiled at Emily. She had short light blond and was well dressed.

"Yes this is my first time in Paris. We arrived last night. I came with a group."

"My name is Helena.""It is a pleasure to meet you. My name is Emily."

There was a silence for a little while then minutes later Emily asked Helena if it was also her first time in Paris.

"No it is not. Every once in a while I come to spend a few days in Paris but I live in London."

"That is nice to be able to visit Paris."

Emily though that would be nice if she could do the same. Maybe one day as spring in Paris is wonderful.

"I hope you enjoy your holidays…"

"Thank you." Emily made a new friend. Then Emily slipped her earphones on. The guide spoke again.

"Ladies and gentlemen. We are entering the elegant Avenue de Champs-Elysees. This is the most famous avenue of the world full of exciting shops and sidewalk cafes…"

Emily noticed it was a good time to take a photo. She walked up to the front of the bus. The view was better as she aimed the camera and clicked twice. Then she walked back to her seat. At that moment the driver drove around the Arc de Triomphe.

Emily took another photo as she saw a good chance they were very close to the Arc de Triomphe. It was wonderful monument and it very large.

Later on they stopped at the famous cathedral of Notre-Dame for a period of fifteen minutes. They stepped out from the bus a few crowds were coming in and out.

Emily walked inside of the cathedral as she walked towards the right side. She saw the stained glass rose window sand they made quite an impression on her. Everything by itself was magnificent. Emily felt the peace of being inside of the cathedral she browsed through. Some of the group was already inside of the bus and others were just looking around.

Moments later everyone was inside of the bus. Afterwards the driver drove away to a different location. They stopped for a few minutes on the Place de Concorde.

Emily asked Elizabeth for her to take a photo of her standing by the fountain. Emily smiled then Elizabeth clicked the camera. It was then time to move again.

After a while Emily spoke to Helena…

"I guess our tour is almost over. It was a pleasure to have met you Helena."

Emily was happy to have met a new friend never known if she might needed any help or someone to talk too.

Helena wrote her London address and the telephone number…

"It was wonderful meeting you."

Emily looked at Helena and then said…"We will be stopping at the Eiffel Tower."

"Yes that is true." Helena looked back to Emily and she asked her if she had any plans for the rest of the afternoon. Emily answered back she didn't know yet as the end of the tour of sightseeing Paris. The double deck bus returned to their location as the tour had finished.

Emily walked around to see if she could find Sarah and Elizabeth from the crowd. She wanted to know what they wanted to do next.

She saw her friends as they were talking with others on their group.

"Sarah…Elizabeth…Did you two enjoy the tour?"

"It was a pleasant and fun. We got to know some of the group. Emily we returned to the hotel for lunch. Do you want to come with us?" Sarah asked Emily.

"That's a good idea."

"Then later we will be deciding what to do after lunch." Elizabeth made a suggestion.

Emily waved goodbye to Helena and she waved back.

Emily and her friends stepped underground. Before going back to the hotel first they had to learn to travel on the metro. They looked at to the large map of the metro system. Then it was easy to get from the hotel or any other direction.

Emily bought some metro tickets so that way it was easy to travel and at the same time very inexpensive.

Moments later they were waiting at the platform then the train came as they stepped in. There were various stops before theirs. Then they walked towards the staircase to the outside. They had to wait for the hotel shuttle bus. Minutes later, the driver stopped then they all got in. Later they all were sitting down looking at the menu of the restaurant. Emily looked at the menu she suggested to her friends to order something familiar.

"You are right Emily." Sarah agreed with her because she knew that her friend was the only there on the group to help them. In that way things would be much easier. They were lucky because Emily under-stood enough for her to order something.

The garcon approached the table to take their order.

"Mademoiselles est-ce que vous etes pretes?"

The garcon smiled at Emily and he politely asked if they were ready to order.

"Oui." Emily smiled back to him and he was very attractive young man.

"Merci Mademoiselle."

It was the middle of the afternoon. When they finished their lunch and afterwards they strolled around the shopping and recreation center where everything was all connected.

Emily walked in to a small jewelry boutique. She browsed a jewelry showcase and she saw a silver heart. She liked it and asked the price and it seemed to be reasonable so she bought it.

"Merci…Mademoiselle."

Then Emily and her friends walked around the shopping center. Afterwards they walked back to the lobby and Emily had no plans for dinner. Meanwhile Sarah and Elizabeth went up to the room while Emily sat down at one of the sofas. Moments, later Miss Stella walked towards to Emily.

"Emily are you alone?" Miss Stella wondered where the other two girls were, as normally she saw Emily always with Sarah and Elizabeth.

"They went up to the room."

"Did you enjoy the city tour Emily?" Miss Stella asked her knowing and for a fact she had loved it. She smiled at Emily.

Miss Stella thought Emily was a very timid student. In her class she did the work and spoke only when it was necessary.

"It was great Miss Stella. I found it a very interesting city."

"By the way Emily would you like to go out for dinner with a few of us. We will take the metro and then we will look for a restaurant."

Meanwhile the other two girls showed up. Then Miss Stella told them to come along too. They immediately said yes and asked what time they would leave.

"How about seven o'clock. We will all meet here. Then we go together by metro."

Everyone agreed. Emily quickly went up to the room. She opened the door and let herself in. She walked to the divan. She wanted to be refreshed a little before going out for dinner.

She was exhausted because she hadn't slept enough the night before. But for her the exhausted didn't matter because she was really happy. Besides there it was a new experience for her. She was glad that her parents had made the right decision of let her coming to Paris. All those thoughts were on her mind as she fell asleep.

When she woke she realized how late it was. Afterwards there was no time to change. She barely had time to touch her face with a bit of make-up. Her hair needed to be done again. Then she twisted her hair into a French twist and tied with a black satin bow. She dabbed a little perfume on her ears and wrists. Then she was ready and she left her room. She stepped out from the elevator and walked towards the reception desk. She handed the key to the receptionist with a smile on her face. He returned the smile and told her she looked great.

At that time everyone was waiting for her. Then they left by the hotel shuttle bus to the nearest metro. The group got off the metro at De Gaulle-Etoille, and they walked up to the street level.

Emily walked to the surface and immediately she saw the majestic Arc-Triomphe. It was a sight to see as they were really close to the Arc.

They strolled for a little while down the Avenue de Champs-Elysees. Then they walked into one of the narrow streets. They began looking for a restaurant for the right price and one in which was open on a Monday evening.

Finally they located one, which suited them perfectly.

"Shall we try this one?"Miss Stella asked. They walked in there was a big group and they choose a long table close to the windows.

Everyone was very hungry and ready to eat. There was the big task of selecting the menu. As there were only two in the group that could translate. Miss Stella and Emily looked at the menu and both read out loud so they could choose something. After a while everyone had an idea of what they wanted.

Three

When Emily arrived in Paris she had no idea how knowledgeable she was on the French language. She began to speak and it came very easily for her. At that time Emily was searching for her deep emotions and at the same time making new friends.

Her new friends seemed to like her company too. She was a very kind and easy person to be around with.

Emily still didn't believe that she was in Paris. It was a dream which came true, and she was feeling great and with a lot of enthusiasm.

Emily chose a French dish and had a mineral water. Usually the dinner took a while before they got served. But it didn't really matter everyone was having a good time.

Afterwards they finished with dinner. They all paid their share and then left. It was a chilly night but still pleasant for a stroll on the Avenue. There were small crowds walking up and down on the sidewalks then Miss Stella asked them if they wanted to stop for coffee for a while. They all said yes.

Emily had coffee but some others had a soft drink. The whole group was having fun they watched the world go by.

After a while they left. They walked down by the stairs to the metro. Miss Stella suggested they visit the Latin Quarter before going back to the hotel. It was one of the interesting areas. They all agreed the time passed quickly then they went back to the hotel.

By the time they arrived it was late. Elizabeth and Sarah walked into the bar to check the scene. Emily went along with the other two.

"Emily do you want to have a coke with us?" Elizabeth suggested.

Sarah touched Emily's arm and said:

"I am tired from all the excitement of today. But I will consider it just for a short time."

Emily smiled the girls went into the bar and waited for a table. The rest of the group followed them into the bar.

Emily smiled to the bartender as she asked for a coke.

"Merci." Then when there was the empty table they moved.

Afterwards Emily sat down for just a few minutes and then got up. She was about to leave but remembered she had to find out the schedule for the next day and she asked Elizabeth if she knew it…

"Elizabeth do you know the schedule for tomorrow?"

But Sarah answered instead of Elizabeth.

"It is a free day."

Emily's money came back to her. Emily walked towards Mrs. King to ask her the schedule. Then she told her she would walk back where the girls were.

"Are you girls all right?" Mrs. King asked Elizabeth and Sarah then answered positively.

"Miss Stella and I we are planning an excursion on the country side. Actually to be precise to Fontainbleau for which we will be taking the train."

Mrs. King smiled to the girls and asked them if any of them was interested in joining them the group.

"All right I will go." Emily answered graciously with a smile. Moments later the two other girls also said yes too.

"We will leaving at ten o'clock. The train ride will be approximately an hour and we will discuss the other details in the morning. Good night girls." Mrs. King left, went to her room.

"Well girls…I am going up too." Emily spoke and then got up and left.

Meanwhile Emily's roommates stayed where they were and they spoke to the other members of the group.

Emily was feeling very tired, as it had been a long day. Minutes later she was unlocking the door and she slipped into her nightgown. There was the moment for relaxing and she turned the lights off. But she left the drapes at the sides. For the moment she looked down below at the street. The traffic noise could be heard up to her floor.

Then she returned to bed and she slipped inside of the white sheets. She searched deeply into her thoughts to let the knowledge that she was really in Paris sink in. What a wonderful thing it would be later on there would be various surprises.

After a while she came back from her thoughts when she heard a knock at the door. Her roommates were knocking very hard-Emily hadn't heard it at first.

"I am coming," she said back to them as she stepped out from bed and went to open the door.

"Thanks Emily." The two of them walked in. As they spoke to her Emily was still out there daydreaming she wasn't fully awake.

"Emily…after you left we met some of the boys from the school." Elizabeth told her with a very enthusiastic voice. Emily didn't responded. Elizabeth noticed Emily was very tired and thought maybe they should discuss on the next day. But she realized that Elizabeth wanted her opinion. So she only asked Elizabeth if the boys were going on the trip on the next day. Then it was Sarah who answered Emily with a yes.

Emily was already in bed when she remembered she had to make a call to the operator for the wake up call but it took only a few moments.

"Merci Mademoiselle…bon nuit."

Gently she lay the receiver down. Then she said good night to both Elizabeth and Sarah. Moments later the girls turned the lights off.

Quickly they had fallen asleep. But Emily lay there sleepless. It took her a long time for her to shut her eyes completely. She searched her thoughts why couldn't she sleep?

Then she remembered it was the espresso coffee; it was strong yet tasted well. It kept her awake all night and finally she had fallen asleep. Dawn came and slowly Emily got up and she wrapped herself with her blue and white robe. She was still feeling drowsy, as she walked towards the bathroom. She turned the faucet onto the right temperature she steps into the tub and left the water running. She stayed for a little then finished her bath.

Minutes later she finished getting dressed she then tied her shoulder length hair into ponytail.

She was stepping out from the bathroom the telephone rang. She knew it was her wakeup call.

"Bonjour Mademoiselle." The operator reminded Emily. Then she thanked her.

"Merci."

She put the telephone down. Emily stepped closer to Elizabeth and Sarah for them to get up.

Finally slowly they stepped out from the beds. Meanwhile Emily prepared her own breakfast; half an hour later the girls were eating too. Emily had finished her breakfast she put everything away in her red Samsonite. Emily was ready then went down to the lobby. Afterwards the other two came down. Already a small group was waiting for the trip to Fontainebleau. Later on everyone was there at lobby ready to leave for the Gare de Lion station.

When the whole group arrived at the station they immediately they checked the schedule for their next destination.

Everyone begin to line-up at the ticket hole to buy the fare. Emily opened her wallet she realized she hadn't enough French francs. She had forgotten to exchange some of her traveller checks.

There was no time for her to go and look for a bank or some agency for change some currency.

She thought, maybe she could borrow some money from Mrs. King. When Emily walked up to Mrs. King and asked her dilemma she said yes. Then she felt relaxed.

The next train was leaving the station in half, which was sixty-four kilometers from Paris. It was a pleasant train ride.

The train arrived at the small station and everyone stepped out the train. Before going anywhere they checked the schedule of the train returning to Paris. It was in the middle of the afternoon.

They all gathered in small groups, they began walking to town. It was a much cool day but very comfortable to walk. The Chateau was a few kilometers away from the main town.

Emily was in one of the groups, they walked to the Chateau grounds. It was the beginning of spring although the gardens were not blowing yet.

Then they walked inside where there were a lot of art treasures. They stopped for a few minutes to observe while Emily was absorbing everything in her mind.

After walking around the halls and looking at pieces of art. They all spent a while then it came the time for lunch. Then they all walked out from the Chateau…

Emily and her group begin walking towards the town. They looked for a place for lunch. There wasn't much to choose but not all went to the same restaurant.

Emily saw one and it seemed all right. There were just a few locals having their coffee. Then Emily walked in and so did the rest of the group. They sat down at a long table as someone hand out two menus. They all were very hungry. Emily had to look at the menu and she helped the others.

But she knew what she wanted, the baguette with ham and French cheese. It was a very typical sandwich but a very filling one. After they finished their lunch they stayed in the restaurant for a little longer, then they left.

They strolled down in the sidewalks and browsed the windows of the small local shops. But they were closed for the lunch they would open again at three o'clock in the afternoon.

The time passed quickly, then it was time to take the train back to Paris. Everyone went back to the station.

When the train arrived at the station and it stopped to get the new passengers. Everyone waited until conductor said all right to step in. After a few minutes they all stepped inside of the train. Emily sat by the window so she could view the scenery the train would go by.

After a half of an hour the train began to move away from the station. The porter then came to check the tickets and punch them.

Meanwhile Mrs. King and Miss Stella were sitting together. They were making plans for the next day as they checked their schedule.

An hour later the train arrived at the Gare of Lion. The whole group walked down to the closet metro. By the time they arrived at the hotel it was late afternoon.

Emily walked to the reception desk to pick up her room key. She went to the room to change clothing and touch up her make-up. She had made plans to meet at the restaurant later on. But there was still a lot time before dinner.

Meanwhile she came down to the shopping center. She walked inside the bookstore. Emily liked to read a lot-it was one of her passions. She took a French magazine from the magazine rack.

She was browsing when suddenly she heard a voice.

"Mademoiselle est-ce que j'ai pouvais aide a vous?" A taller young man asked,as he had recognized her a tourist.

He was a very handsome young man. She looked at him and immediately she saw his baby blue eyes. Right away there was some attraction for him. Emily smiled she said.

"Merci monsieur." He tried to find out where she was coming from. Although she spoke French but she was for sure the foreigner. He tried to talk to her that time with a different approach.

"Peutre c'est votre premier fois a Paris?"

She couldn't say no that time…

"Oui."

He turned around and then presented himself…

"Je m'appelle Pierre." He smiled to her. Then she responded to him.

"Enchante Pierre. Je m'appelle Emily."

That time they seemed to get their feet straight on the ground. She looked at the magazine and she made up her mind to buy it. Of course he offered to buy it. But she didn't accept it. She walked to the cashier and then walked towards Pierre. She began a conversation with him. She told him she was having dinner with her friends. Then he asked her she would accept a coffee with him at the coffee shop in the shopping center.

"Oui bien."

They walked into the café and they sat down their table overlooked the inside of the shopping area. Then out of the blue he spoke English. Emily was surprised because she was not expecting it.

Right away they were some kind of attraction between them. They admired each other's eyes. Emily felt a warm feeling coming from Pierre. But at that moment the garcon brought their coffees. This was a happy moment for Emily as she was enjoying Pierre's company even if it was for a short while.

After finishing her coffee it was time to leave. She thanked Pierre and then walked back to the hotel lobby uncertain of seeing him again.

The girls were at their usual place, which was at the hotel bar in the lobby.

"Wait a few minutes and sit down, Emily. We will go in the little while."

Of course she sat down and she wondered why she came to the exact time they had planned to have dinner. She could stay with Pierre a little longer.

Finally they were ready to leave for dinner. It was just around the corner of the lobby. The maitre d' showed their table but Elizabeth saw some of the others sitting along a table. But there was still enough room for them. Then she asked Emily to ask the maitre d' if they could sit at their table of their friends. Then they all sat down. Meanwhile Emily browsed. But she looked at the menu she decided to have something very French the garcon took her order and after all it didn't take too long for her to be served.

Suddenly the group sitting on her table, became very noisy,.

The maitre d' approached the table. He spoke to Emily and asked her to tell them to quiet down. He began to speak with Emily and after a while she found out that he spoke the same language.

Emily looked back at the day. She remembered having a fantastic day in the countryside. When she went to search her mind remembering seeing a movie at the same Chateau, which she had been in that day. She had moments, she was alone with her thoughts.

Minutes later she finished her dinner. Then she went for a stroll in the shopping center. Emily sometimes felt a bit out of place being much older than the rest of the group and later in she ended up at bookstore again. She browsed between the shelves and then chose an easy reading romantic book. Then she looked through she knew it she could read it and it was simple. Then she paid for it. Then went into the same side café where she had been earlier.

Then the garcon approached the table.

"Oui Mademoiselle."

"Un cafécafé s' il vous plait." Emily asked politely for a coffee. A few moments later the garcon was at her table.

"Merci."

Emily was looking around idly when she saw Pierre. He couldn't see her.

Meanwhile Emily finished her coffee then left.

She returned to the hotel. She looked around for her friends afterwards she peeked and saw them at the bar. She said good night to them. Then she took the elevator up to the room. Emily was exhausted after the long day. Moments later she was undressing and feeling comfortable.

She lay quietly in bed and read a few pages of the French novel. After a while she had given up on her reading. She was tired and couldn't stay any longer awake. By the time the other the two other two girls were at the door. Emily was fast asleep and they were knocking at the door.

But Emily couldn't hear a thing. She was in the deep sleep.

After a few minutes they were knocking hard at the door without any reply. Elizabeth went down to the reception desk to get a supply key. Elizabeth turned the key and opened the door. Sarah walked in while Elizabeth took back the key to the receptionist.

Soon both the girls were fast asleep.

The new day began with the traffic noise just below them. Then the telephone rang a few rings before anyone picked the receiver up. Slowly Emily got up from bed and answered the telephone.

"Oui." Emily responded."Bonjour Mademoiselle."

"Merci."

Quickly Emily picked her makeup case and chose something to wear. Before she went to take a shower she looked at the window to see the weather. It seemed there were a lot of the clouds around and it was chilly.

She chose the warm sweater and her casual pants. She had a good night's sleep and she was feeling better. She rushed herself to get ready. She was unusually behind that morning. Emily was the first one in bathroom. She was almost ready but her roommates were still in bed. She wasn't surprised, it was always like this.

Emily shouted out for them to get up "Elizabeth…Sarah…get up…it is time…"

They moaned and again turned before they really got up. Meanwhile Emily prepared her own breakfast. She sat and then moved the coffee table closer to her and she ate one croissant. It was a very lousy day to go on a boat ride. But they didn't have a choice every day they were in Paris there was always some place to go and see.

Already it was in the middle of the week and the time seemed to pass very quickly.

When Emily stepped inside of the cruise boat she chose to stay in the open air while others stayed inside. Everyone else preferred looking from inside out

Meanwhile Emily felt some rain drops on her face because she had a headscarf. She stayed where she was. Afterwards the little drops stopped.

Emily took a few photos of the sights. She was just passing by the Notre-Dame Cathedral. It was then, she asked a person close to her to take a photo.

"Thank you." She said and then he smiled back and said…

"Welcome."

Paris was a city full of beauty and so much history. The cruise boat passed under the many bridges. Each one had some significance. The morning went quickly, as they went back to the point where they had started.

Afterwards they separated in small groups and went into their different ways. A few went to the Eiffel Tower, which was very close by. Meanwhile Emily went to a different direction with her small group.

They took a metro and they went to the Gallery of L'Afayette. Emily was passing by a small shop in which she bought some film and afterwards they stepped out in the street. There were a lot of shops in the street.

Emily noticed a familiar chain store across the street the Marks and Spencer but she didn't go inside.

She wanted to buy something for her father. Emily and her friends walked inside of men's shop.

Emily browsed it and saw a silk tie. Then she bought it.

Afterwards they all went for lunch and luckily there was one restaurant close by. They all went in the place was full there was a waiting time before they had a table.

They had a wonderful lunch and then the afternoon got brighter and much warmer. They walked around and Emily saw an American Express travel agency where she needed to exchange some travel checks.

She walked in and went to the information booth. They directed her to the second floor.

She walked up one floor her friends follow her. But there was a small line-up

It didn't take long and soon she called out to her friends

"All right let's go. I am going to buy a few postcards for a keepsake."

Emily looked around the postcard rack and picks just a few. She went to the cashier.

"I am done, shall we go?"

At that time they were close by the Opera de Paris, where they had been earlier in the week. On that occasion they were touring the city by the Cityrama tours. They recognized the area. They began to walk around to see the interesting shops.

One of them stepped inside of a shoe shop and all went in to browse for a little while and then they left.

After a wonderful afternoon of walking the streets of Paris. Emily and her friends went back to the hotel. Emily had done her shopping and she bought also some souvenirs for her.

She had gone to do her shopping at Au Printemps and the Galeries Lafayettes both were in the boulevard Hausmann. When they arrived at the hotel Emily went to the reception desk for the key of the room. She walked towards the elevator and pushed the up button.

Moments later the elevator door opened she stepped inside. The elevator was about to close someone shouted out to hold it.

"Une minute s' il vous plait." The Frenchman rushed in and then the door, closet it.

Emily looked and couldn't believe her eyes. She was in luck when she saw who it was.

"Bonjour Emily. How are you?"

He spoke to her with a French accent. She couldn't believe her eyes he was so close to her and there he was in which made her very happy. He looked at Emily with his baby blue eyes and he was well dressed.

"I am fine thank you." Emily answered. He reached over and kissed her on her cheeks.

Pierre realized Emily's happiness. She brightened up she smiled at him and her eyes sparkle.

"I see you are happy to see me." Pierre smiled back to her. There was some kind of attraction just there between the two of them. But the elevator stopped at her floor.

"Pierre…this is where I get off. How about meeting me later in?"

Emily stepped out from the elevator.

"Oui Emily…how about in ten minutes in the lobby."

Emily was radiant with happiness then smiled at Pierre as the door closed. She walked around the corridor until she was in front of her room. When she unlocked the room she saw that it had been cleaned. She walked in and then took her red Samsonite from the closet. She opened it and took out what she needed it.

Emily quickly freshened up and then put away her purchases. She twisted her hair in a French twist. She had adjusted her look for the evening. She was in the bathroom when suddenly she heard a knock at the door.

She stepped out from the bathroom and opened the door. The two girls were standing there…

"Hello Elizabeth…Sarah" Emily then closed the door.

"Is everything fine with you?" Sarah asked Emily.

"Yes I think I am making progress in a relationship."

Emily began talking with them but she was in a rush.

"I will be meeting him in a little while."

Emily slipped into her two-piece outfit.

Elizabeth walked up to Emily and asked her if she had any plans for the evening.

"See you two later I will have dinner around seven o'clock." Emily left. A few minutes later she was looking for Pierre. But she had no idea what was the evening schedule. She wondered if they were dining out. She would know the evening would progress. The evening was still early and she looked around to see her new friend. But instead she saw one of her teachers. She asked her what their evening plans were.

Mrs. King said they were going to the casino Lido to see an evening show. Then right away Mrs. King asked her if she wanted to go with them.

"Yes Mrs. King…I would like to go."

Then asked Mrs. King what time they were leaving.

"We will be leaving around nine o'clock. The show is at ten o'clock."

"I will be here at that time."

Meanwhile she sat down on the round sofa waiting for Pierre. Maybe he hadn't understood her she thought. But she waited for him.

After a while she was tired of sitting. She got up and walked towards the restaurant so she could have dinner. She was about to ask the maitre d' for a table herself.

Sudden she heard someone calling her.

"Emily…ma cher amie pardonnez-moi." Pierre approached her; he was late. He asked her for forgiveness. He had been detained for a lot longer than he had expected.

"Of course," Emily answered back saying everything was all right. Pierre asked her if she wanted to dine somewhere else.

"Oui."

She told him she had to be back to the lobby at a certain time. She was meeting her friends there. Pierre agreed. Then they walked out holding hands. There it was the beginning of their friendship. They walked to the bistro. The décor looked very French and the setting was a very romantic. They spoke for a little while she was glad that Pierre had brought there. By each table there was a rose in a vase. The bistro was very close to the hotel, which made everything easier. They were comfortable just being there the two of them. They were sitting in one of the private spots away from action of the bistro. Pierre put his arms around Emily's showing his romantic feelings.

Emily didn't want to have any alcohol.

"Pierre I will have a Perrier." He chose a house wine. Meanwhile Emily spoke about her favorite things, like what she wanted to do in her time in Paris. So far she was very much enjoying herself. Then the waiter at that instant brought their hot plates, which it smelled very good.

Emily was then ready to eat she was hungry. Anything she ate and made her feel, good. After a while they both finished dining. Then there was time to leave Pierre took her back to the hotel. They walked and held hands.

Suddenly Pierre just stopped walking. Then paused for a moment, embraced her and then their lips touched.

Emily heart began to pump faster he went deep inside her lips. She felt a great sensation, as she had not been kissed with so much passion before. She leaned into Pierre's arms. They let themselves go. Pierre asked her if she wanted to go up to his apartment, which was near from where they were.

Emily said almost yes in her mind but in her heart was no. Maybe it was too soon and anyway she had to be at the lobby of the hotel.

"All right Emily." He understood. It was close to the nine-thirty. Then further along the way Pierre stopped again. He noticed it she was shivering with cold. It was a bit chilly and she had long sleeves but it wasn't sufficient. So he took his gabardine and wrapped around her.

"Merci Pierre." She thanked him she felt much better and warmer. But before going anywhere Pierre embraced her tightly and kissed her deeply. Emily felt wonderful and very happy.

She was beginning to have feelings for him.

Emily was beginning to fall in love with Pierre. Their attraction was bigger each time they saw each other. They walked the rest of the way holding hands and they arrived at the hotel. They walked to the lobby they both sat down.

"I don't know if I will see you tomorrow. Will I?"

"Oui ma cherie." Emily talked about her trip. It would take the entire day.

They agreed that they would see each other in the evening. They would get together they kissed goodwell bye and then left.

Emily stayed until she saw Elizabeth and Sarah.

"Emily are you coming with us tonight?" Sarah asked her and the rest of the group was gathering around. But Emily told her friends she was going up to the room to get her coat.

"All right Emily goes quickly. We will be leaving soon."

"Yes." She got the key from the reception desk. Minutes later she was opening the door. Then she brushed her hair and slipped a bit of red lipstick and rouge on her face. She took her coat from the closest and then left.

A few minutes later she was in the lobby. The group was ready to leave. They stepped into the shuttle bus the driver left them at the metro. Since a few stayed behind then the first ones waited underground in the metro.

Meanwhile Emily talked about her dinner she had with Pierre to Sarah and Elizabeth. There were a small number of them listening to her.

In the group there was someone named Donny. He attended the same highschoolhigh school as Emily. He was in the same grade but in a different class. He was looking at Emily a lot his eyes didn't seem to be anywhere else but on her. Finally the whole group had arrived so they could go together by metro. A few minutes later everyone stepped inside of the train.

Later, they all stepped out towards where the casino Lido was located. But was it turned out that there was a bit of time before the show. They all walked to the café across the casino. There were a lot of expensive cars parked in the street. The huge group all went in and they had to pull a few tables together then sat down. Everyone had something; some had coffee and others had soft drinks. When it came time for Emily to pay her share someone had paid already. She had no idea whom, had though.

He kept it secret. There were a lot of thoughts bouncing in Emily's head. If she thought about it; it might be Donny. But she wasn't sure at all.

Then it was time to leave to go across to the casino. Everyone was holding, there own show ticket. Emily walked by the porter and he cut the ticket in half.

"Merci Mademoiselle."

Then she walked up to the second floor where the garcon showed her seat. Then Emily tipped him.

"Merci Mademoiselle."

Minutes later everyone was in theirhis or her seats. The lights dimmed the music began and the curtains slowly risen. The chorus girls came out one by one into the stage. All of them had a different costume and all of them were topless.

Emily heard a few giggles and saw the girls laughing. She looked at them and they stopped they realized they were making fools of themselves. The quieted down and for the following performances they were silent.

Afterwards a magician performed some magic and another few acts came to the stage. After a while there was an interval of fifteen minutes before the second part of the show.

Emily stayed seated while the other got up and walked outside in the main foyer.

A fifteen minutes later the lights dimmed and the music began. Everyone returned to theirs seats. An hour and a half later the show was over. They walked out from the casino.

All of them had a long walk. After midnight they arrived at the hotel. They all were very exhausted and the next day would be a very busy one.

Emily walked to the receptionist for the key and they all went to their rooms.

She opened the door the two followed her and then close the door.

"I hope you girls are tired. I am very tired."

Emily made a telephone call to the operator for the wake up call.

Moments later the two were in bed. Emily at that time was the last one. She lay there under the white sheets; to her it felt very good. Her body was all in pain from walking all day.

A few minutes later they all were asleep.

Her mind wondered all night dreaming.

It took her along time for her to fall asleep. But she did. The few hours of the night were passing quickly. Then the morning came and so did the traffic. But somehow that morning was very difficult.

Emily turned and rolled until she heard the telephone ring. She knew it that it was time, to get up. She felt a little bit chilly. Then she lifted the receiver.

"Oui."

She still had a sleepy voice…

"Bonjour Mademoiselle il estest. huit heures."

Emily replied in French.

"Merci Madame." Then she really noticed she was running late that morning. She walked towards the bathroom stopped by their beds and touched their shoulders.

"Come in girls. It is time to get up."

Then she stepped into the bathroom and quickly took a shower. She felt awake and refreshed. The night had been short. A few minutes later she was dressed with her sporty clothes. Then she wrapped her scarf around her neck. Then she stepped out. The girls were still under sheets. By then it was really getting late…

"Come in Elizabeth…Sarah." While the girls got ready Emily made her breakfast.

Five

The day passed quickly and then it was time to meet Pierre.

"Voila ma petit apartment Emily." She didn't find it at all small which it looked very comfortable.

She was impressed. "Assez-vous." Emily sat on the sofa. Meanwhile Pierre turned his stereo on to listen for romantic music.

Pierre asked her if she wanted something to drink. She said a mineral water would do fine. He took two glasses with a piece of lime in and ice then he poured her water. It was really late and Emily was beginning to feel exhausted. But she didn't want him to notice. It had been a long day and after all with the sound of music it made it easy to be sleepy.

There was the opportunity for Pierre to make love to Emily. But it had to be the right moment. Pierre came closer to her he began kissing her. They both really got into the mood. Emily felt something really wonderful.

It was the first time of her life she was being involved with someone like Pierre.

She hadn't encountering that feeling before. He sat in the sofa and gently bent over to kiss her in the lips. Then slowly they both embraced. He was in top of her and Emily didn't mind all. He kissed her as she had never been kissed before. Pierre was a wonderful kisser and he kissed her deeply.

Pierre had entered into her soul no one had done. She was wonderful and had so much passion.

She wished she could stay longer in Paris. Even, if that was the beginning of spring and a very chilly one. She felt wonderful and just a few days being Paris. Emily didn't believe that she was Paris. A very exciting city to be in love and so many places to enjoy. They were both deeply involved.

They lay quietly together for a time and Emily fell asleep in Pierre's arms. When he noticed she was sleeping he gently lay her down in the sofa. Then he pushed the sofa bed out. He took her shoes off and pulled a blanket over her. She didn't felt anything, he turned the music off and the lights too.

Then quietly he put everything away and got ready to go bed.

He slipped into his shorts and under the sheets he went. His thoughts were in, Emily he fell asleep. The room was dark meanwhile Emily slept and after a few hours she woke.

Emily felt very uncomfortable being dressed. She undressed and took a slow walk around the apartment.

The room was dark except for a little light coming in from the street through the window. She eventually went back to bed.

After turning a few times she finally fell asleep. Before dawn Pierre got up he wrapped himself in a silky red robe. He stepped into the bathroom and then checked to see if Emily was all right. He had notices that her clothing was in top of the chair. There was a lot of temptation to slip under the sheets with her again. But Pierre backed away from that idea. Then he walked back to his room. He began dressing in something causal. Afterwards he went to the kitchen to prepare le petit-dejeuner for both of them. It was really early in the morning and Pierre tried to be as quieter, as possible.

Suddenly Emily was awake. Pierre walked to the sofa gently he came closer to her and spoke.

"Bonjour ma cherie Emily. Comment ca va?" Emily smiled back to Pierre.

"Bonjour Pierre. Je suis bien merci."

"Voila ma robe Emily." Responded. "Oui

"Un moment s' il vous plait Pierre."

He understood what she wanted from him. He turned around and walked to the kitchen. When she was alone she wrapped his robe around her. Pierre told Emily where the bathroom was and quickly she took a shower. She felt fresh. She slipped back her teddy and wrapped his robe around her body.

She went back to the living room and still felt tired. Then she walked towards Pierre he was preparing breakfast. He had fresh croissants and sweet tasting bread.

He was brewing the fresh pot of coffee. He had set up already the table. Pierre asked Emily to sit down for breakfast as he brought the tray with everything to the living room table.

Emily hadn't had a breakfast like that for so long, everything had done in a special way. After eating the fresh croissants Pierre asked her she wanted more café au lait. He then poured it into her cup.

Pierre put down the coffeepot. Then he came closer to Emily and put his arms around her. He kissed her slowly. They both were involved.Pierre gently touched her face as his lips touched hers. Then he began to make love to her passionately. She had never been loved that way before. She felt wonderful for her that was the first time ever. What a lovely moment to be in love in that romantic city! All kinds of thoughts went into her mind if she was doing the right thing.

He knew how to please her. Then Pierre said to her.

"Je t'aime ma Cherie." She lifted her head and smiled and said. "Moi aussi."

After a while they both decided to get dressed. Pierre wasn't working in that day. Emily also had no plans for the day but she wanted to know what the rest of the group was doing. They went back to her hotel and Emily walked to the reception desk to ask for the key of the room. She picked the key up and Pierre stayed in the lobby. Then he walked to the bar while Emily went up to the room.Emily opened the door and the room was not cleaned yet. But she saw a written note from the girls.

""We hope you had a good night Emily. Today we have a free day. There were no plans so we went by metro to look around. See you tonight, Emily, and have a pleasant day with Pierre.

…Sincerely, Sarah and Elizabeth."

Emily stepped inside the bathroom to touch up her make up. She brushed her and tied her hair into a ponytail. Then she decided to change the clothing for something more comfortable. She slipped into her casual pants and matching top and the sweater. Then she took her leather jacket in case there was a chilly air.

Then she wrote down a note for the girls. "To…Elizabeth and Sarah. Thanks girls for the nice note. I will be spending the whole day with Pierre. I will see you both tonight."…

She left the note on the dresser. She walked out and locked the door. Quickly she pushed the elevator button and a few seconds later the elevator door opened. She stepped inside of the elevator and minutes later she was in the lobby. Then she walked towards the bar.

There he was in the bar talking to the bartender. They knew each other; his name was Jean. Emily sat at the bar…

"Oui Mademoiselle." Jean asked her if she desired something.

"Non merci."

At that point Pierre interrupted…

"Mademoiselle Emily…Ella etait avec moi. Jean."

Emily smiled to Pierre then said.

"Nous pouvons allez parce que tout va bien." Then Pierre said. "Bien."

Then Pierre got up and so did Emily then they begin to walk back to the entrance. Jean said good goodbye to both of them.

"Au revoir Pierre Mademoiselle." Pierre then said. "Au revoir Jean." They walked out holding hands, it was still morning but the morning went fast. It was time for lunch.

"Nous allons quelque place dans la rue des Champs d'Elysees autre place Emily."

"Oui Pierre bien." They both were smiling to each other.

Emily was feeling so happy and she had never felt like that before. There were no words to explain how she felt and they walked two blocks before going down to the metro.

Pierre was going to show Emily all the sights of Paris, as the weather was all right and only a little bit on the chilly side. But the sun was shining and then they stepped underground to the metro. There was any kind of business underneath the city. Emily saw a bank counter where she wanted to exchange some currency. She then asked Pierre to wait a minute she wanted to go to the bank. She exchanged two travel checks.

Moments later she was again besides Pierre. Then they both waited at the platform for the train to arrive. They stepped inside of the first class, as it was only a little more expensive. Pierre had paid for the tickets he always liked to travel first class. They got out at the Rond Point des Champs d' Elysees.

They walked to the Bistro de la Gare. By then both were very hungry they walked in the restaurant. The maitre d' showed a table for two and Pierre asked Emily if she wanted any wine with her lunch. She wanted just a glass of red wine and she chose a lean grilled beef salad.

Both were enjoying each other company and they spoke quietly. Once a while they held their hands. They finished their lunch with fantastic desserts. They tasted incredible. It had been a marvelous lunch with the best company she could ever asked for it. After a wonderful dessert they had a French style coffee. Later the two walked out from the bistro, walked for a little while, then took the metro. They got out to the closest dock, as they would be taking a cruise in the Seine. They sat down for a little while and Emily was amazed at herself. Her expectations were higher. She loved, speaking the language and Emily had been in a boat tour before with her group. But that was different from being with someone special. . Afterwards they took the metro from Pont de Alma to the Avenue des Champs-Elysees. They walked towards the Avenue until they found the place they wanted. Minutes later they found an empty table and sat down. The garcon came over to their table.

"Oui Monsieur."

"Deux café au lait s' il vous plait."

Minutes later the garcon brought their white coffees. Slowly Emily sipped her coffee, as she held it in her hand. They laughed with each. Pierre teased her kissed her.

He said to her that he had a surprise for the evening.

She wondered what he had in mind.

"Chere Emily j'avait une surprise pour vous."

"Pour moi Pierre?"

"Oui Emily."

But he didn't say anything else. The time passed quickly and Emily knew it was time to leave for the hotel. Pierre took her back then and he left her at the lobby. He told her they would meet in two hours.

Emily looked around to see if she would see her friends. She went to the bar, which she saw they're both there.

"Where have you been?"

"Here and there."

"How are you?"

"We are well…how are you Emily?"

She smile back to them as she was happy…

"I had a marvelous time last night. I stayed over to Pierre's place. Today we had a marvelous day in Paris. I came to change my clothes then afterwards we will go out for dinner."

Emily sat besides one of the girls. She asked the bartender for a mineral water. They talked for a while meanwhile Emily asked the girls what their plans for the night. They would be spending a few hours in a nightclub. Then they would returns to the hotel before one o'clock. She told the girls about what kind of the day she had.

Emily face was radiant then it was time for her to change again. She would be going out for dinner with Pierre. Then she said…

"See you tonight Elizabeth and Sarah." Then she walked to the reception desk and asked for the key.

"May I please have the key for the room 305."

The receptionist had her the key…

"Merci monsieur."

Emily walked to the elevator and pushed the up button. She stepped inside but as soon as the elevator door was closed. Suddenly it opened again the group of Japanese students rushed inside. The elevator was full. Everyone was squeezed like lemon. She had never seen something like that before. She got scared and as soon as the elevator stopped at her floor she got out. She was glad of it.

Emily went around the corridor then opened the door and then it. She was tired and she sat down in the divan she wanted to rest for a little while. Her feet were desperately tired and a little bit swollen.

She took her shoes off and she felt better. She rested a little bit it had been along day. She only needed to rest a little bit.

Her journey to Paris was almost over. It had gone really fast although the days had been wonderful. A wonderful evening was waiting for her and she didn't know what was going to happen. She hoped always for a romantic one.

It would be one of the last nights in Paris. She would not forget, as long she would remember. She closed her eyes for a moment her thoughts were on Pierre. He was very attractive to her. Maybe it was his blue eyes and his rosy cheeks. There was the physical attraction between her and Pierre. She dozed off for a while without any notice. Then there was a knock at the door. At first she didn't hear a thing. Then a male voice spoke…

"Mademoiselle. Mademoiselle!"

There was then a moment of silence. Emily finally heard the voice behind the door.

She quickly got up and rushed to the door to open. Then she opened and saw a young garcon in uniform. He was the hotel gofer he had a box in his hands wrapped up with a pretty red bowl.

"Mademoiselle…Emily."

Then she closed the door and sat down and opened the package. Her face lit up with the purest of joy for inside was a pretty dress. It seemed to be a perfect fit. She took it out from the box and she felt the fabric-silky cotton with a tiny print. It was a very feminine outfit, cut at the waist with long sleeves and knee length. She read the note in French.

"Emily ma Cherie je vous aime beaucoup." She took the dress and slipped it on.

It fit just right. Then she applied a little bit of rouge in her cheeks.

Then the last was her hair. After a few moments she was ready she went down to the lobby to meet Pierre.

She wondered after all she was just going though a crush or if it was real. Maybe it was the surroundings, after all it was spring in Paris. Emily stepped out from the elevator she met Elizabeth she was going to the room.

"Hello Emily. I am going to change my coat."

"Here it is the key Elizabeth."

She looked at Emily then she said.

"You look great. I see you are going somewhere and I don't have to guess with whom. Pierre of course."

"You are right Elizabeth."

"Thanks for the key I hope to see you later Emily." Elizabeth touched the elevator button. Emily found one empty spot and sat down waiting for Pierre.

"Her thoughts were far away and she wondered what her parents would say about the relationship with Pierre.

Maybe they would be disappointed or maybe not. She hoped they understood her feelings. After all it was her first time out alone away from home. She was old enough to make her own decisions.

However sometimes they would meddle in her personal life.

She remembered the announcement of the trip, which everyone was excited about it. Emily right away assumed she would not be going but to her surprise, she did. Here she was in Paris and having a wonderful time.

After all those thoughts she came back to the present. She saw Mrs. King at that point who came over to talk to Emily.

"How are you Emily?" Mrs. King was always concerned with her students.

"I am fine thank you."

"Have you been enjoying the trip? Oh! I see you have a lovely dress. Are you going out this evening?" Emily thanked Mrs. King for her kindness. She explained she was going for dinner with a new friend. After a while she left.

Emily was alone once more and was waiting for Pierre. She began to worry as she saw the time passing quickly. He did not seem to be near at all but he couldn't do that to her.

Emily got up for a little while she began to be restless. She saw her friends passing by and going into different directions. After all he must be coming soon at least she hoped so! Suddenly she felt a hand in her shoulder she turned around and saw Pierre. Her face lit up with joy and she smiled.

Then they embraced and he kissed her in both cheeks. The evening would be a memorable one.

Pierre smiled to her as his eyes met hers. They knew it that was their moment.

"Bien Emily. Est-ce que tu etes pretes?"

"Oui Pierre. Nous pouvons allez bien j'aime cette marveheuse robe merci Pierre."

She thanked him for a beautiful dress. They moved along and he took her hand and he held it very tight. They walked out into the street.

The night was warm enough to be outside. It was not cold and the sky was clear stars could be seen all around. It was after all a romantic evening for lovers to walk by each other side.

Pierre waved his hand out to go get a taxi. Moments later they were inside of a taxi. He told the driver to show her some of her sights so

they could see Paris by night. Every important monument was illumi-
nated and Paris was completely different from day to night. There was
something about Paris at night, full of lights, the crowd expressing
their feelings more freely!

The driver stopped at the restaurant they would be dining at. Emily
stepped out from the taxi then Pierre paid the driver. For a moment
they stood there and his baby blue eyes met hers if it was for the first
time. They smiled at each other and they had a sparkle in their eyes.
Pierre took her to him and his lips met hers. They kissed passion-
ately-there was so much electricity between the two of them. They
could hardly contain themselves. Emily's thoughts were flashing back
and forth as their hearts were touching and their minds connecting.
"Oui…ma Cherie. C'est cette soir."
"Bien Pierre ma amour."
They knew that they would make love that night. They were ready
and willing. Pierre opened the door for her and she walked in first.
Pierre followed her and the maitre d' showed their table. He seemed
to know Pierre by the way they communicated.
"Bon soir Pierre."
"Pardon moi mademoiselle." They follow the maitre d' to their table.
"Bien Pierre."

"Merci." Both were comfortably seated Emily looked at the menu. By
that time she was beginning to get hungry. It was already late in the
evening but she chose something light. She felt a tingling feeling; she
wanted more from Pierre than she was admitting.
Emily was beginning to fall in love with Pierre.
He was kind and gentle as they toasted each other.
Their dinner came to an end then they left the restaurant. They
walked outside towards a narrow street and Pierre took Emily's arms to
hold her tight. Then he stopped, and kissed her deeply.

Afterwards they walked again until a taxi driver took them back to one interesting place. The driver stopped at a small hotel-it was out of the way but a very nice place. Pierre had made a reservation earlier the room had a great view to the whole city. The city was illumined in the evening, which made it very.

Emily was very surprised, as he was very romantic had a bouquet of fresh flowers on the table and a bottle of French champagne chilling.

They stepped out to the balcony. Emily couldn't believe her eyes-this was why Pierre had been late

When Emily looked outwards she saw the Eiffel Tower all lit up and the surrounding beauty all around. Pierre was just behind her and he held her tightly.

He began to whisper to her ear.

"Bien Emily. Est-ce que vous aimez cette grand image?" He was asking if she liked the view.

"Oui Pierre. C'est fantastique."

Then he turned to her. He picked the bottle of champagne and the cork popped out into the air. He got closer to her. Then he poured the champagne into the long glasses. He handed in a glass to her and held one for dinner. They made a toast to each other and Pierre quickly finished his glass while Emily sipped hers slowly. Pierre walked to the light switch and it turned it off. There was only a soft light on he stepped into the bathroom.

He quickly refreshed himself and a few moments later he came out. Emily wanted this to be very special night. She would not forget this for along while.

He had prepared the night with every little detail. He had bought a beautiful nightgown and a matching robe for her. He had hoped she liked it as he left the small wrapped package with a nice print paper. He left the package in the counter of the bathroom with a simple written note.

"Ma petite cheri Emily…de votre amour Pierre."

Moments, later Emily went to the bathroom and saw the package and read the note. She felt his warm she slipped it on and it felt right. She let her hair down and she dabbed a little perfume and rubbed a little bit of hand cream in her hands.

Emily took a few minutes for herself and pleasant thoughts went through her mind. There was no turning back and she hoped the evening would turn out well. She was positive about it. Pierre was the man of her dreams she had come a long way for someone special. It was important for her that she made the right decision.

All that was in her mind that moment was there. Emily came out from the bathroom the room was dark.

Pierre had turned the lights off but there was still light coming from outside through the window.

Emily walked slowly to the bed. She slipped underneath the warm sheets.

Emily could feel Pierre's warm body getting closer to hers. "Oui ma cherie Emily."

He embraced her and then they were touching each other.

There were no words to describe what she felt. She couldn't resist him, he was so powerful over her. They made love to each other. He tried to be gentle with her. She felt his tenderness love and pleasure as. She had never before. She wasn't afraid of him and he tried not to hurt her he was gentle but at the same time very physical. Both were very quiet there were no words between the two of them until much later.

"Oui Emily. Je vous aime mom amour." He kissed her and wrapped his arms around her body.

He didn't want her go. He pleaded with her to stay in Paris. They would work something out if she really loved him. She couldn't stay. She explained everything to him she would come back in the summer.

They would write to each other.

"Oui! Mon cher cette ete." Emily didn't wanted to remind herself that she really had one more day to stay in Paris. She wanted to remember those moments and be happy for a few ones.

Emily spoke softly to Pierre…

"Oui Pierre. Je t'aime beaucoup aussi."

After those romantic feelings they fell asleep in each other's arms. Soon the night had turned into the hours of the morning. The dawn arrived the dlight crept into the hotel room. Then they were awake.

The wonderful feelings were still there in each other faces. There were really spring and romance in Paris.

"Bonjour Emily." He smiled at her and kissed her gently on her lips.

"Oui bonjour Pierre. Ca va bien?"

"Oui ma cherie." He wrapped his robe around himself then walked out to the balcony for the fresh air and the view of the city. It was glorious no matter if was night or day.

Emily was surrounded by all kinds of fresh food. All the different smells were outside from different places. She began to desire a lavish French continental breakfast. All those delicious hot croissants with lots of butter as tasty could be. All of these were in her mind.

"Yes the continental."

"Oui café au lait." Emily liked that idea indeed.

After a long night a nice breakfast would be fine. She came inside and Pierre was already coming towards her. He asked her to sit for le petit dejeuner. Minutes later someone was knocking at the door.

"Oui."

"Entre vous s' il vous plait." The garcon left the tray in the table and then left…

"Merci."

Pierre sat down and they both began to eat. She was busy eating and had a lot of her thoughts about her day. They finished breakfast Pierre got up and sat by Emily's side. He took her hands and told her to stand up. Then he led her to the balcony so she could see the Paris and remember him. She looked out to the city and the view was a memorable one. It would always be a special place as they stood there in silence. Suddenly she was in his arms again there were feelings, as they were close.

They hadn't dressed yet so they stepped inside. Once more they began to make love and there was so much passion. But out of the out of the blue Emily broke away from Pierre. She couldn't go any longer, she began to feel a pain in her heart because she was not sure she would ever see him again. At that moment Pierre questioned her actions. Emily tried to explain to him with so much sadness in her eyes and her heart. But he understood her feelings-she was leaving soon, yet he was staying.

Emily stepped inside the bathroom. She washed herself she came back a few moments. He asked her if she was feeling better.

"Oui Pierre. Merci"

They sat for a little but soon it was time to get to get dressed and leave for the hotel. Meanwhile they agreed to meet for dinner at the hotel. She left Emily kissed Pierre, both said au revoir for that moment. They seemed to be content. Emily walked by one of the narrow streets until she stepped down in the metro. A half of an hour later she was asking for the hotel key at the reception desk.

Minutes later she changed her beautiful dress for something more casual. Then she left. Emily was proud of her beautiful smile. She made others feel good.

"Bonjour Mademoiselle. Bien tous."

Emily smiled and responded to the receptionist.

"Merci Monsieur."

Afterwards she walked outside and waited for the shuttle bus to take her to the metro. It was day in Paris. It was after all a very bright and wonderful morning. She was feeling better ad she was going to visit the Louvre. It was very busy being a Saturday and there were crowds in every corner of the museum.

Emily walked slowly and observed the many famous paintings from the old masters. She stopped to looked at the famous Mona Lisa and it was true what they said had said. No matter which view you looked it seemed she was looking back at you. It was what the master Leonardo intended when he painted the Mona Lisa.

Emily paused for a few moments then she walked around to observe other paintings. It would really take days to see the whole museum but she had a few hours.

Her intention was to visit the museum and other places afterwards in the summer.

She was looking at one of the paintings when she saw Elizabeth and Sarah and some other friends.

"Hello Elizabeth…Sarah. How are you two doing?"

"Ah! Emily it is nice to see you at last!"

"I am fine thank you." Sarah didn't speak a word but stood there looking at Emily.

Emily asked them if they were staying long at the museum.

"Emily we will be visiting for the rest of the morning and a bit of the afternoon. Do you like to stay with us?" Elizabeth and asked her.

"Elizabeth I will be here for a while then I will return to the hotel went to a different area to a another time in history. The impressionism period was one of Emily's favorites. Monet was the painter she admired the most. One of her favorites was the huge panel of lilies.

Emily tried to see much she could in a short time. She wished to go back one day to see Paris. She fell in love with the romantic city.

It was around two o'clock in the afternoon she decided to go back to the hotel. She was beginning to feel hungry and she needed to eat something.

She walked down to the nearest metro. Since was close to the museum the platforms were full of statues which it was very unique way to point the way from and back to the Louvre.

Emily was by herself so she took the metro. But somehow she got on the wrong train by mistake. As Soon as she realized this she went back to the right one. Finally she arrived at the hotel. She asked for the key of the room at the reception desk. The other two had not yet arrived. She was feeling tired anyway. She wanted a few moments by herself because she was so exhausted. She pushed the elevator and ready to go up. Suddenly the elevator door opened and a whole group of Japanese students went rushing in. Everyone was squeezed like sardines. Emily stayed calm as the same thing had happen once. As soon as her floor came the elevator opened and she excused herself in French. She stepped out from elevator. Then she went around until she got to the room. Immediately she sat in the bed she was very exhausted. So her body was saying something else at the same time she was hungry. She soon fell asleep.

It was around one hour later when she was awakened by the noise from the street below.

The police passed by in the hurry with the siren in.

Quickly she got up and went to the bathroom for a quick shower. She would feel fresher and much awake.

She came down to the restaurant at that time she was famished.

She chose spaghetti with meatballs.

The restaurant was practically empty and she was enjoying a quiet moment by herself. She had a wonderful tasty au café at the end of a great lunch. It was Emily's last day in Paris. But she still had to pack, which wouldn't take long.

Emily decided to leave at that point as the maitre d' approached the table. He said good-bye to her; he had been very friendly to her. Minutes later she walked out from the restaurant. She walked to the shopping center. She browsed in the boutiques, then walked into the bookstore. She looked at the French magazines and at the same time she looked to see if she could see Pierre.

But she didn't have any luck. Afterwards she went in to the café and she sat down.

The garcon approached the table.

"Oui Mademoiselle."

"Un café au lait s'il vous plait."

"Bien."

Meanwhile she looked at the magazine. The time were really passing quickly she would be missing Pierre. But she had to leave.

She will not forget a wonderful week she had in Paris. Suddenly she heard a voice calling her.

"Mademoiselle votre café au lait."

"Merci." She thanked him slowly she sipped her French coffee. She took another glance at the magazine. By that time it was close towards the evening.

Emily finished her cup of coffee then called out the garcon to pay. Then she left. She walked back to the hotel then asked the key of her room. She went up to her room and began pack her clothing. It didn't take her too.

Afterwards she brushed her hair and touched up her face with a little make-up. Then she felt better. She closed her luggage and put it away then it was time to leave. Then she heard a knock at the door she opened to see who it was. There they were Sarah and Elizabeth.

"Come in." She smiled to them.

"I was about to leave."

"Emily did you had a nice afternoon?" Elizabeth asked her.

"Quite a wonderful and relaxing one." She responded to her and then left. Before leaving she left the key with one of them. She told them she had finished packing.

Moments later she was sitting down in the sofa in the lobby. She had no idea if she would see Pierre again.

If she would see him it would be her last evening together. After waiting a while she went into the bar and she asked for a Perrier. She was terribly thirsty it must have been the spaghetti she ate.

The bar wasn't full. Since the bartender knew Pierre, she asked him if he had seen him around. He had not seen him.

Then she left the bar. She went to the restaurant there was a few groups sitting at the tables.

Some she knew and others looked familiar to her. A group, which was in one of the tables called her to come to sit by their sides. Emily accepted their invitation.

"Emily come on sit by our table," one of the girls called out loud.

"Thanks." Emily polite thanked them. She didn't mind all being by herself. But who knew what it would turns out to be that evening. Maybe it would be something different than she would expect.

The whole group was just beginning to have dinner. The waiter showed her a menu she looked carefully to see what she would like. She chose one omelet with ham. The waiter took her order.

"Merci Mademoiselle."

They asked Emily if she wanted to come with them to a discotheque for one hour or two.

"All right I will go with all of you. But I won't stay long."

Emily knew that the next day would be a long one. They would be travelling all day. They waited for Emily to finished her dinner. Quickly she ate and they were ready to leave.

They all walked out from the restaurant. Emily excused herself for five minutes to get her coat.

Quickly they left the hotel by the shuttle bus. Then they were in the metro and when they got to the discotheque it was still closed. All of them waited outside until they opened the doors. The group got bigger and bigger everyone was laughing and talking out loud making new friends from all parts of the globe. When it became time the door opened the place was full. Emily sat beside someone new whom she had met outside.

She had a Coke and some of her friends went to the floor to dance. She waited for someone asked to ask her to dance. Then a few moments later someone asked. Then she smiled and said"Oui.""Bien Mademoiselle." So a young man with curly brown asked her for a dance. He seemed to be from another country originally. He was pleasant to talk to. They dance for a while then both sat down with his friends. He asked her if she wanted something to drink. She thanked him but didn't want anything.

Emily asked what was his name. He told her…

"Je m'appelle Filipe."

Fillipe asked her for another dance and she accepted. But soon it was time for her to leave.

"Au revoir Fillipe."

He kissed her and wished her well.

"Au revoir Emily."

Emily's group was waiting for her she was taking her time. A few minutes later they left they walked to the metro. A half an hour later they arrived at the hotel.

Emily went to the bar. The rest of them all went up to their rooms. She saw, the girls amusing themselves then Emily approached. She sat down for a little while. She wondered if the girls had packed yet. Sarah answered Emily.

"I didn't yet. It will take a few minutes." "Well I packed." Emily was glad she had done all her packing. It was already midnight and Emily wondered if she was going to see Pierre again. The other two decided to go up to bed. But they had to pack quickly.

"All right I will see you too later." Elizabeth and Sarah left.

Meanwhile Emily stayed a little longer. But she walked to the lobby area she sat down in the sofa. The crowds were getting smaller and smaller. Everyone was retiring for the evening. She was about to give up. She felt a hand on her shoulder she turned around saw Pierre. He was just standing there. He smiled at her then he kissed her right cheek. He whispered to her with his French voice.

"Emily viens ici avec moi." She followed him outside but inside of the shopping center. It was serene and so peaceful and a perfect place to be romantic it was the right spot.

Pierre knew there was no crowds at that time. He pulled her towards him. He embraced her tightly. He kissed her deeply; their passion seemed to grow as they saw each other.

It was the last night together and she was not sure what the future would hold for her. No matter how she would find a way. After that night they will not see each other. But Emily didn't want that to happen and she must think of something. What she had in her mind it was to come back again perhaps in the summer or the fall. But for her the ideal time would be in the middle of the month of August.

All her thoughts were in her mind and at the same time she was having so much pleasure with Pierre's company. He was kind to her; they wanted again to make love to each other. She knew that her friends were not sleeping they were packing. She came back to reality then Pierre mentioned for them to go to the coffee shop.

"Bien Pierre nous allons."Emily sat down while Pierre went to the bar.

He said something to the waiter. She was guessing that he was ordering two, café au lait. Moments, later Pierre sat besides her.

"Oui c'est la vie mon cherie. C'etait au matin que vous allez partir? C'est ca?" She responded to his question it would be in the next morning they will be leaving.

"Oui? C'etait demain au matin." He held her hands tightly.

"Vous etes triste n'est-ce pas ma petite cherie."

"Oui Pierre. Mais c'etait moment je suis tres heureuse." She was happy she had met that wonderful gentle young Frenchman.Emily felt attracted to his baby blue eyes. His face so rosy by itself it was an unusual feature. Her thoughts were pouring into, her mind. Her first true love it was so important to her. She had always thoughts in her mind. She came to realize that Pierre was getting closer and closer to her. He kissed with deep emotion. Then the garcon excused himself and he left the two café au lait and plate with various delicious pastries.

"Merci…merci." They said at the same time that was the surprise for Emily from Pierre she smiled.

"Oui c'est ma surpris? Oui, Pierre. J'aime les petites gateaux."

Emily tasted one of the pastries. A good treat to have to end the evening.

Pierre helped himself too. He liked also sweets. They finished the whole plate and it was time to leave. The time was passing quickly for Pierre and Emily. They walked back to the hotel; there was so quietness all around. At that moment there was no words to express their feelings. It was a late and it had been a long day. Before they got to the lobby they made a lot of stops.

Emily pushed the elevator button.

Pierre led her in moments later they were at the right floor.

Emily knocked at the door and Sarah came to open the door. They were finishing packing they were surprised that Emily came with Pierre. They went in. Emily presented Pierre to Sarah and Elizabeth.

"Bon nuit Elizabeth…Sarah. C'est une plaisir."

"Well it is nice to meet you Pierre." Elizabeth said, as she was much more out going than Sarah.

Elizabeth was closing her luggage Sarah had finished earlier. She lay there in her bed. Then Emily asked her if she was tired.

"Are you tired Sarah?"

"I am and I guess everyone is-all the excitement of the week. We won't forget for a long time."

Then Emily smiled although she was so tired and then said.

"I am sure of that for me it couldn't been better."

Emily was so happy as she had Pierre at her side. Her eyes were lit up with so much joy. Her happiness was coming from within. The girls were about to party a little longer in one of the other rooms with another group.

"Emily…Sarah and I we will be joining some other group next door. Would you like to come with us?"

Elizabeth asked her and of course Pierre can come along too. Emily was about to ask Pierre about the time beyond last night together.

"All right Emily…See you later." The girls put their baggage away then they left. Well they were alone again. Pierre took off his raincoat they seemed to be comfortable. Emily was tired she hadn't to many hours of sleep.

The night was going to be different. They turned the lights off. The only light coming through was from the street below. There was a silence all around. Emily sat in the bed and Pierre came over. They were both at ease with each other. They didn't speak at all and they were in each other's arms. Pierre deeply kissed Emily.

Pierre held her hands tightly and he said something to her.

"Oui ma cherie cette nuit c'est la derierre nuit. C'etait au revoir."

"Oui mon amour. Mais…"

At that moment there were no more words for long time. They felt at ease with each other. Pierre pulled Emily towards him. They kissed gently he undressed her and at the same time he took his. They deeply kissed they lay in the divan. They rushed beneath of the white sheets the room was quiet. They were making beautiful sweet love.

Emily knew it these lasts moments were so precious to her. She had never felt that desire the first time ever so important. She was feeling the spring air in Paris. She hadn't planned to feel like that in any way they were deeply involved with each other.

Emily forgot everything especially she was about to leave in a few hours. She was living the marvelous city of Paris behind.

Their passion was very powerful, their hearts were burning until the last moment. They kissed in each other's arms. Pierre didn't want to let her go. They were underneath the white linen but still composed they lay there. They fell asleep close to each other in the small space.

She was dreaming about the wonderful person whom was by her side. Emily heard a knock at the door she forgotten about her friends. At that moment she dropped all her thoughts. There it was the second knock at the door a tiny voice said.

"Emily is us please open the door."

Emily quickly got up and she slipped her robe she was by the door.

"I am coming." She opened the door and the girls walked in.

"I am sorry and I heard the first knock."

"It is all right."

"We had all so much fun we talked about each others plans for the summer."

"I am glad"

"There was a small group some from others schools. Anyway we both had fun. I see Pierre is still here."

Sarah said back to Emily.

"He fell asleep." Emily told Sarah but she didn't wants to say anything else. She didn't want to give any satisfaction to her. Emily then pulled the drapes so they could sleep a little better.

She checked everything for the departure. Then she tried to squeeze into the divan. She tried to forget everything and to sleep for a few hours. But it seemed impossible she was beside Pierre.

The room was dark there was a silence. Soon she fell asleep a couple more hours passed into the morning. The operator the called the room.

It was still along way from the busy hours of the morning. When the telephone rung a few rings. Emily picked the receiver up and answered it. She knew who it was she then thanked the operator.

"Merci." Emily stayed up and then she began to get ready for the trip back home. A few minutes later she said good morning to Pierre. She wondered how he slept; it was uncomfortable.

"Bonjour Emily…Comment va cette matin?"

"Je suis bien merci."

Pierre kissed her slightly in her cheeks then let her go. Emily walked to Elizabeth and Sarah she told them to get up.

"Good morning it is time to get up." One of them…

"One more minute."

Emily wasn't surprised at all. Every morning since they had arrived in Paris they were hard to get up from bed. But she didn't leave them alone. Emily finished to get ready. She decided to have her breakfast downstairs in the restaurant. But she had to be sure both of them were really up.

"Sarah…I think we will have ours here. We are running a bit late."

Meanwhile Elizabeth was in the bathroom.

"All right see you both in the lobby."

"See you later Emily." Sarah said back.

Emily was ready she picked her belongings, Pierre helped with her luggage. They left Emily went around the corridor.Pierre pushed the elevator button then stepped inside. Moments later they were in the lobby.

Emily left her red luggage besides the others to be loaded into the charter bus. Emily and Pierre walked to the restaurant it was full. But there was one table for two. Emily sat down and quickly looked at the menu she chose the continental breakfast. She loved those French croissants with lots of marmalade and the café au lait. A few moments later they were eating Pierre held Emily's hands. They knew it there wasn't much time left. There was a lot of movement about as the groups were getting in the lobby.

Almost every group was gathered in the lobby to listen to the last minute information before departing.

Elizabeth and Sarah had come down the teachers were busy checking out all the names in the list. Mrs. King checked Emily name in the list. Meanwhile the driver was loading the baggage into the bus.

Then it was time for everyone to step inside of the bus. But before she went. Pierre held her hand he led her behind the bus. They didn't spoke a word, there was no need for it, they, knew it. They had to express their own feelings.

There was no time to talk Pierre pulled her gently towards him. They were close to each other.

Pierre kissed her deeply. There were no words, to describe what they were feeling at that moment. They kissed for the last time they were so much in love and had so much desire to stay together.

Then they came apart from for a quick moment until they embraced once more. He promised to her he would write, then Emily walked to the front of the bus. They both waved to each other.

"Au revoir ma cherie Emily. Bon voyage au revoir."

He said that out loud and waved back. He blew a kiss. Emily said with a sad voice still smiled to Pierre.

"Au revoir Pierre…Pierre." She wished she could have said something else.

Emily was the last one to get in. She sat beside the window the driver was ready to leave.

She looked through the window as Pierre stood there he waved to her. She waved back and her thoughts was in him she said to herself…

"Je t'aime Pierre. Nous pouvons voir une jour nous allons voir."

Then the hotel was out of sight.

The driver would take the same route he had before. It was very early in the morning time passed quickly. Although it was a long drive it was quite different from the time they came. The weather had changed drastically. The driver would drive north towards Belgium. It were getting colder suddenly it began to snow. After a while really got bad and which it made the journey harder but the driver stopped two times in the way to Holland until their destination to the Amsterdam Airport.

Some how it seemed, a very long way back then they had the flight hours to bear again. It was a few longer. They were some glad to go home and others they wished it were a little longer. They had to go back to their classes everything would return back to normal.

Nine

Finally they had arrived at the airport. There was a huge crowd Emily had her long winter coat because was so chilly for the time of the year. The driver stopped at the main entrance of the airport. Everyone stepped out of the charter bus. Meanwhile the driver unloaded their baggage then each of them picked their own.

Emily looks out for her red Samsonite. She went to the checking counter there was a huge line up. It had been a very exhausting morning. After a long wait everyone was checked in.

Then it was a departure time and they walked the long corridors towards the plane.

Emily was happy and at the same time was emotional. She was full of excitement because of the tremendous week. Everything was turning to fast she hadn't expected. They all were seated in their seats. The pilot spoke and shortly after he took off. Emily was happy she walked around the aisle up and down talking to her fellow passengers.

It was one easy way to pass the time.

Finally they arrived at their destinations. Emily passed quickly through the Canadian customs. Then she said goodbye to her friends she would see them in a few days.

Emily was happy to be back home. She walked out through the electronic doors. There were a crowd waiting for the passengers arriving from the Amsterdam flight.

She looked out there to see if she would see her parents. Minutes, later Emily was embracing her parents Emily's sister was also standing there too with her son John. He was happy to see his aunt.

She was happy to see them but she was very tired.

"Hello papa…mamma. How are you both?"

"Hello sister…little John."

"We are all glad to see you Emily." Her father said to her smiling at her he embraced her.

"Emily you must be very exhausted from the journey."

"I am really tired. I could use some time relaxing but it was worth after all."

"Let's all go home. We had dinner before coming to the airport. Your nephew didn't like the place."

"John are you all right now you can tell your auntie Emily?"

"Right…Auntie Emily."

"Good."

They all walked towards the elevator and they pushed the number eight. The crowds were enormous everyone were trying to move out.

Finally two hours later after her arrival Emily was at home.

She sat down in one of the lounging chairs in the family room. Everyone joined her all wanted to know about her trip to Paris.

Emily politely told them there was plenty time. She needed to rest.

"All right Emily. I will hold until tomorrow."

Her sister was really nosy she wanted always to know everything.

But Emily wasn't about to reveal her happiness yet. Her mother asked her if she wanted anything to eat. She was feeling hungry for homemade food. She asked her mother I she had any of her favorite soups.

"Yes dear. I will go warm up some."

"That I will make me feel good mamma."

"I will call you when the soup is warm."

Emily sat down her thought were on Pierre. He was so far away in the another continent. She was missing already him very much. She held to her memories. They were strong enough to hold by the huge distance between them of two.

"Emily…the soup is ready." Her mother called out."I am coming." Emily got up and walked to the kitchen, which was not too far away. Her nephew was playing with the boys he had his pajamas on in.

It was time for him to go to bed. Meanwhile his mother was writing the letter to her husband.

"Thanks mamma." Emily began eating homemade soup. Her mother watched her daughter eat she sat in the opposite side of the table.

"Emily did you really enjoy Paris?" Emily's mother wondered if it had changed since she was there a few years earlier with her father.

"I love it very much. There were days that it was in the chilly side. But the French are really great. I haven't had any problems trying to communicate in French."

Emily tried to finish eating so she could go to bed. She was exhausted. Then, said to her mother.

"Mamma I feel very tired I will go to bed."

"Yes dear that is a good idea. You must rest."

"Good night sleep well."

A few moments later she was in her room. Quickly she was in bed and it didn't take long for her to be asleep. Emily's body was full of aches and pains from sitting down too many hours.

She tried to imagine being in Paris with Pierre. A lot of hours passed until the morning and she awoke on her own. After a long rest she felt very much rested and felt better. She came downstairs to the kitchen. Her mother was preparing some of the ingredients to bake a cake. Her father had left for the office her sister went at shopping mall close by. But her nephew was watching the cartoons in the living room.

"Good morning mamma. "I slept really well. Where is everyone?"

"Your father have left and your sister went shopping."

"I am famished and I will make a big breakfast."

Emily helped herself. She made a fresh pot of coffee while her mother was still in the kitchen baking a cake for John and the rest of the family.

Her nephew came running to the kitchen as he had heard voices.

"Hello auntie Emily."

"Good morning John. Do you like to watch cartoons?"

"Yes I like it."

"Do you want anything to eat? Auntie Emily is going to make something to eat."

"Toast with butter please."

"Okay if you want to go back to watch the cartoons. I will call you when it is ready."

John went running back to the television. Meanwhile Emily made breakfast and half an hour later Emily and her nephew were eating.

Emily's mother was checking the oven to see if the orange soft cake was ready to be taken out from the oven. At the same time Emily's mother was making conversation with her daughter.

"Are you ready to talk to us about any details from your journey?"

"Mamma…I will talk to you later in but for now. I am still thinking about Paris."

"It seems you must have had a good time there?"

Emily had decided that she wasn't going to tell her parents yet about Pierre, especially her mother. She would tell them after she received any letter from Pierre. Otherwise there would be a lot of time. She wanted to look for a job. So she could earn some money for her trip back towards the end of the summer. But there were her studies to finish. She still had two days before going back to school again.

Her sister was staying for two more weeks before going back to her husband. Emily was in her last year of her high school. She still wasn't sure she wanted to go to college or university. But she had to make up her mind very soon. Emily liked the arts so she could choose something in the fashion field.

After her breakfast she played with her nephew for a little while. He was the only nephew she had.

Three hours later her sister arrived from her shopping. Emily's sister wanted also to know details about her trip to Paris. But she told her only that she was returning to classes in two days.

That afternoon she went to look for a part time job. She applied to various places one of the places was a clothing shop. She would be waiting for their answers.

Later she went home.

In the middle of the week she went back to school. She had studied very hard to get good grades. A week passed and she received a telephone call from a shop. The answer was a positive. She could start her job the next day. She was happy since she found the job. The days she didn't had school she would have more hours. She needed the money for her expenses.

By the time her sister had left, there had not been any communication with Pierre. Every night when she went to bed her thoughts were always in Pierre.

She was getting disappointed she hadn't told her parents. There was no point to it. Weeks had passed and spring was about over and summer had arrived. The days were warmer. She still had her job she had finished her school year.

She was working full time.

Ten

It was the beginning of the month of July. One day she was coming home after her job, her mother handed her a letter. She glanced at it and immediately she saw that it was from France.

She was very tired and she went right away to her bedroom. Before going up she thanked her mother.

"Thanks mamma. I am going to my room. I am tired, we had a very busy day in the shop. We had a lot of sales. The shop had these great sales in two pieces outfits and a lot of swimming suits too."

"Good night Emily. Is that letter from your friend?"

"Yes mamma. Good night."

Emily went up to her room. She had been standing up all day and moving a lot. The only rest was in her lunch and dinner break. She closed the bedroom door then she jumped into bed.

Quickly she opened the envelope and right away saw that the letter was from Pierre She began to read the two page's letter. She had given up but everything had changed. Her heart began to beat faster as she wondered if the letter would bring her bad or good news. Emily began reading the letter, which it was in French…

"Ma petite cherie, Emily. Je suis tres triste avec moi-meme pour n'est pas de vous ecrive.

Quelque chose arrivais avec moi famille. C'est que une chose terrible. Tout le temps je suis.

Etait occupe avec cette probleme. Mais je n'est pas obliee de vous ma cherie. Comment

Ca va vous?"

Mais maintenant tous va bien avec moi. Je pouvais visite vous dans une mois de l' aout…

Je vous aime mon amour Emily…

He was upset with himself for not writing to her. He had a problem with his family. But now everything was all right. He would be visiting her in the month of August. He asked how she was. He loves her very much.

She finished reading the letter and at the end of written pages. He signed his name and pledges his love to her. She felt that it was enough reason to forgive him. She would try to write back to him.

After finishing Pierre's letter finally she fell asleep feeling better.

The weeks passed she wrote a few letters to Pierre. He wrote back. Finally she was ready to talk to her mother and father about Pierre. Her intention was to go back to Paris to take a course in fashion design. Afterwards find a part time job in the same field in one of the houses of fashion.

Emily had saved some money for the trip and some extra to use for a while. But the best time for her it was the end of the summer. On that weekend she spoke to her parents. They said it was all right with them and asked her if she needed any kind of help. She responded, to them if she needed any she would ask for it. She thanked them for their help and understanding her situation.

One day she decided to call the French Consulate for some information about the French schools and other information relating to her trip back to France.

Two weeks later she had a large brown envelope with all kinds of booklets.

She looked at everything and found out, what she needed. She was doing well in work. Later towards the end of the month of August she began preparing what she needed for the departure to Paris.

Emily wrote to Pierre about her news she was returning to Paris towards the end of the month of September.

She would keep him informed in any news. Pierre then wrote back he was happy with the news and asked if he could help her in any way.

She told him she would like him to make some reservations in a small hotel. But to wait until she had the flight ticket. Emily asked her father for a favor. She needed a good travel agency where she could purchase her ticket. She didn't wants to be misled. He suggested her to take her mother to see Paris and at the same time meet Pierre. She could stay for a period of two weeks.

"It is a good idea papa…mamma would love to see Paris. I am sure."

"Then come with me so we can purchase the tickets."

"Today I have to work all day but I will ask for two hours off tomorrow."

"Then we will see my travel agent tomorrow if it is all right." Emily went to work that day. She spoke to the manager and she said yes. But she had to work the follow day and she agreed. She was much happier. Although she, missed Pierre.

She didn't mind her father's suggestion. The next day her father drove her to see his travel agency. At first she didn't like any of the places to stay. But she kept looking and she finally found a place. The place was around the Avenue of Opera and the price was right too.

Then she wrote to Pierre to tell him to make reservations. She told him her mother was coming for two weeks. Emily got a quick response from Pierre. Everything was all set she had nothing to worry about. The past months she had not had any social life at all. She had been occupied with her work.

The time was approaching more quickly. Her mother was also preparing for the trip. They both went shopping and she paid even for some of Emily's clothing. She was nice to her daughter.

One day Emily came home after working all day. She was happier.

"How are you dear?" Her mother asked her as she handed out a letter from Pierre.

"I am so tired today. We had a tremendous day in sales."

"I have good news for you. I hope it is a letter from Pierre."

"It is good news indeed."

Emily went in to her room. She got ready to bed. Then she opened Pierre's letter. She was happy to receive his letter.

"Bien cherie Emily. Je suis heureux parce qu'il a peu jours pour voir vous mon amour.

J' espere que votre famille va bien. Tout ici va bien aussi.

Je pense, que vous etait heureuse pour voir moi.

Bon c'etait tout pour maintenat.

Je vous aime beaucoup Emily."

She felt better there were a few weeks left for her departure. In her free moments she began to organize her clothing and any other things needed.

She had read the letter, which had mentioned that he was happy because there were a few days.

Before, he would see her. Everything was all right there. That was everything. He loved her very much.

Her mother was also a very excited too; they were going to enjoy each other's company.

The next day Emily wasn't working and they went shopping.

"Good morning mamma. How are you this morning?"

"I am well thank you. How about you?"

"I feel well this morning. Mamma are we still going shopping today?"

"Yes if you are up to it."

"Fine with me mamma."

"Do you anything to eat Emily?"

"It is all right mamma. I will make something. Then we can go afterwards."

"Okay then. I will go to get dressed while you eat."

An hour later both mother and daughter drove away. After a while of shopping both went for lunch. Their relationship was in better terms than before.

"Emily are you ready for the trip? I am very happy that you chose me to go with you."

"Yes mother. I have picked some of the fall clothing. The manger helped me choose the pieces of clothing."

"That is good Emily. Then you are set."

"I am glad we chose today to come shopping as it gives us a chance to be together."

"I feel the same."

"Did papa mention anything about you going to Paris?"

"He is happy and I am glad you wanted me to come too."

"Did you choose yet? The waiter is coming to our table."

"I will have a salad platter."

"I think I will have the same."

The water approached the table to take their order.

"Are you ladies ready to order?"

It didn't take long for them to be eating. The waiter served them quickly and after a while they both left. Afterwards they went back shopping and they had finished for the day. They left and went home. Her mother opened the door and let Emily in first. She closed the door.

"I am getting started in dinner."

"All right mother. I am going up to my room to put my purchases away."

There were two weeks before leaving for Paris. Emily began to sort out her clothing. There was a lot of packing to be done. She didn't know when she would be back. She came down just a few minutes before din-ner. She helped her mother to set the table. Meanwhile her father arrived from work. Moments later they all were having a nice dinner as they talked about the trip. All they talked about Paris.

A few days had passed and Emily was all packed and she had the plane ticket. Both mother and daughter were ready for their marvelous trip.

Finally the departure day arrived. Emily was very enthusiastic about it. The flight was in Sunday afternoon. The whole family went for a late lunch at one of the restaurants close by their house.

Her mother would return in two days weeks. When they returned from the restaurant the two travelers checked to see if they had everything.

Afterwards they left for the airport. There was a huge crowd at the checking counter. But soon was their turn.

Eleven

After a long wait they both had good seats. Her father looked at her and wondered if she was nervous.

"Emily are you nervous to meet Pierre again?"

"I guess I am a little bit. But I am glad the day came."

"How about you dear?" Her father asked her mother wondering how she felt leaving her husband behind.

"I am glad that I am travelling with my daughter. You will be okay dear. It will be only two weeks which will pass quickly."

"Right dear. You are right. I will still be missing you."

"Yes that is sweet of you honey."

"Emily I hope everything will turn out well for you."

"I hope so papa. We will call you. Mamma will tell all the details afterwards."

"I hope you two have a nice flight to Paris." They said their good bye. Her mother embraced her father and kissed him on both cheeks. Moments later Emily embraced her father and then said…

"I will take good care of mamma."

"I am sure you will Emily."

"Bye papa. "Good bye honey." Her mother said back to her father and blew a kiss. They both walked around the corridor towards the departure area. They sat down and waited until the airline would call by intercom.

"Emily is Pierre waiting upon our arrival?"

"No mamma. He will meet us afterwards in the lobby of our hotel. He is working."

"Anyway it is all right."

"We will take a taxi from Galle airport to the hotel de Sege."

"Right."

A few minutes later the airline called the passengers. They began the long walk towards the entrance of the plane. Emily sat by the window and left her small handbag underneath the seat.

She tried to be comfortable for the long voyage overseas. After a long while every passenger was settled in.

Moments later the captain began speaking to the passengers.

"Ladies and Gentlemen we will be taking off in a few minutes. We are waiting for our turn to take off. I hope you all enjoy the flight."

"Moments later the runway was clear for them to take off. Minutes later the plane was up in the air. The flight attendants were serving drinks while the passengers enjoyed their drinks then the flight attendants prepared the dinner trays.

It was very dark and after dinner there was a moment to relax and for some sleep.

"Mamma I will be closing my eyes for a moment."

"Yes Emily. I think it is a good idea. I will try to do the same."

Emily was beginning to shut her eyes as, she couldn't resist any longer. But a while later she did fall asleep. The flight was coming towards an end but still a while before touching down. The flight attendants began to serve breakfast.

"Honey are you feeling better?" Emily's mother asked her. Then she smiled and said with a gentle voice.

"Yes now that I slept a little. We will approaching Paris is in hour."

"This is been a good flight so far. After we get there we will just rest. We have to get used to the different time zone.

"It will at least take a two days before we get settled down."

"Yes."

The time was getting shorter as they were really close to Paris. Emily excused herself she went to the tiny washroom to touch up her face. She never knew if Pierre could be at the airport. Pierre sometimes surprised her.

Emily came from the bathroom and then she looked at her mother and asked her.

"How do I look mamma?" Her mother smiled at her and she said she looked wonderful and rested.

"I will go touched up too." After a few minutes later the captain spoke…" Ladies and Gentlemen we will be landing soon in Paris. I hope you all enjoyed the flight. We hope to see you soon. Thank you."

Her mother sat down. Then the fasten seatbelt sign came in…"This is it." Her mother said it she held Emily's hands for support.

"I am a bit nervous mamma. I know that I am seeing Pierre soon."

Emily's mother exclaimed to her…"You love him. I can see in your eyes. I am happy for you."

"I am glad mamma. Thanks for feeling that way."

The captain spoke moments later again. He announced.

"We are flying over Paris soon we will be landing."

The passengers sat by the window had a great view from above. They saw Paris by air and it was a beautiful sight; the morning seemed to be a clear one and it wasn't cold at all.

Finally the plane touched down. It took a few moments until the passengers began to get up from their seats and gathering their belongings.

Emily and her mother were very happy for their arrival in Paris. They walked towards the officials and they had no problems. Meanwhile they waited for their baggage.

"There is our luggage."

Emily had spotted their luggage right away and walked towards the electric belt. Her mother also helped her.

"I know you are very anxious to get out of here." Her mother knew very well, she was looking forward to see Pierre as soon as she could.

Emily looked around for a porter to help them with the baggage. They had a few pieces to carry.

"Monsieur s'il vous plait." The porter quickly handled their baggage.

"Bien Mademoiselle." They all walked towards the doors, which took them outside. Emily asked the porter for a taxi.

"Oui Mademoiselle." He responded politely to Emily's request.

"Merci."

The porter waved to a taxi…

He loaded the baggage and Emily's mother stepped inside while Emily tipped the porter.

"Merci Mademoiselle."

Then Emily got in the taxi and as she didn't seen Pierre she would go straight to the hotel.

Emily told the driver where she wanted to go.

"Oui Mademoiselle."

He really took off fast. Her mother "Emily they do drive fast here and dangerous."

"Mamma you will get used to it."

"This is just a breathtaking. I love it already." Emily's mother said with a very enthusiastic voice. She was happy coming along even leaving her husband for a while.

The taxi driver spoke to Emily…" Le hotel de Sege."

"Merci."

The driver stopped at the hotel. They stepped out from the taxi and the driver took out the baggage. Then a porter came right away to pick them up. Emily paid the taxi "Merci Mademoiselle."

Emily walked to the reception desk and she checked in. A few minutes later they were in their room. It was a nice room and they liked it. Then Emily tipped the porter with a few francs she had.

"Merci Mademoiselle." The porter closed the door. They were left alone.

Emily began to settle down and she changed into her comfortable clothes. Her mother noticed a lovely bouquet of fresh flowers in a vase with a card.

"Emily looked what is on the table."

Emily picked up the card…"Bienvenue a Paris mon chere Emily."

"Pierre sign his name."

"How lovely it is for Pierre to send these beautiful flowers. "Emily smelled the flowers as she then kept the card close to her heart. She smiled. But they were still had jet leg.

"Mamma…I am going to lay down to rest for a few hours. Then we can go down to the restaurant or maybe some where else for dinner."

"Yes Emily. Meanwhile I will unpack. Then I will try to rest too."

Emily pulled some of the curtains and lay in one of the twin beds. Then she pulled the blanket over her.

Moments later she was in her deep sleep. Her thoughts were on being in Paris. She was anxious to see Pierre as she was feeling so much passion towards him. She wanted to touch and kiss him. His love was so wonderful and it was worth waiting for. So she wanted the time to pass so she could see him.

Meanwhile her mother unpacked some of her belongings. Then she tried to rest also for a while too. There was silence for a while and the time passed quickly.

Emily had rested well and then she was awake and then took a shower. It was already the middle of the afternoon and it was getting closer to the evening.

Emily took her time in the shower; she used her favor French Lancome gel, that, had brought with her. She stepped out from the shower and dried herself and got dressed. Afterwards she went down to the lobby to see if there was any message for her.

Meanwhile her mother was still resting. She checked at the reception desk there was no message. Then she went back to her room to prepare her handbag for the staying in Paris. She had a few francs left but she needed to exchange some currency.

Suddenly her mother was awake from her nap.

"Emily did you have a good rest?"

"Yes mamma. I feel much better now."

Her mother wondered about Pierre if Emily had received any news..."Any news from Pierre?"

"Not yet."

"Emily he will probably show up don't worry. Meanwhile I will call your father so he will know everything is all right. Emily do you mind calling the operator for me?"

"Not at all...I will do it in a moment."

Later both were on the telephone. Emily spoke to her father then handed in the receiver to her mother.

They both were on the line for a few minutes. Meanwhile Emily came down to the lobby to check some information in Paris. Then she asked the receptionist if there were any restaurants close by the hotel.

She wrote them down in her notebook and then she walked towards the elevator and pushed the button.

Suddenly she heard a male voice asking about a guest staying at the hotel. Then she heard said they were in room 202. Emily realized that it was her room number.

Emily looked back and saw Pierre. She smiled and called out a loud his name...

"Pierre...Pierre. C'est moi Emily."

She walked towards him and moments later both were in each other arms. They kissed deeply and their warm feelings came to the surface. Emily felt relief at seeing him as it had been so long. Pierre came apart from Emily, then he held her hand they stepped inside of the elevator. The door closed.

Pierre embraced Emily and then spoke.

"Ma cherie Emily je t'aime...il etait beaucoup de temps de voir vous. Mais maintenat vous etes ici."

"Moi aussi Pierre. Je pense que nous allons passe beaucoup temps avec vous."

"Nous sommes maintenat tres heureuses."

"Oui Pierre."

Again they kissed. She felt wonderful being in with Pierre. The elevator door opened they stopped at the right door.

Emily knocked at the door and her mother answered then she opened. They walked in. Then Emily had introduced Pierre.

"Enchante Madame. C'est un plaisir et bienvenue a Paris."

"I am glad to be here and it is a pleasure to meet you at last."

They got to know each other then Emily suggested they all go out for dinner. Pierre knew a small restaurant not too far away. They walked to the restaurant and had dinner afterwards they walked back to the hotel.

Emily's mother made the suggestions to her she could stay longer with Pierre. She was going back with the key. "Good night mamma."

"Good night Emily and tell Pierre good night for me."

"I will tell him."

Emily came down to the lobby and she sat beside Pierre. They talked to each other. She told him that her mother had said good night to him. She was feeling tired and needed her rest. They went to his hotel room

They made passion love and Emily could hear his heart beat. They both fell asleep in each other arms.

A new day began the sunlight came through the windows. Emily felt the warmth of his arms around her. She was glad that he was beside her. She looked at him and saw he was still asleep.

Silently she got up and went straight to the bathroom for a shower.Moments later she came out from the bathroom and still he wasn't, awake. Then she called the reception desk to order breakfast for two. Emily bent over Pierre then whispered in his ear…

"Bonjour mon cherie."

"Bonjour ma Emily vous etes bien?"

"Je veux tres bien merci."

Pierre held Emily hands as he smiled at her. She was feeling wonderful and it was beginning of something good. She hoped to find work she needed and at the same time find a place. But if she didn't find something she would have to ask Pierre's help. All those thoughts were in her mind. She heard a knock at the door. It was the garcon with a tray full of fresh croissants coffee and all others wonderful goodies. She signed the bill and tipped him.

Pierre was in the bathroom taking a shower. Quickly Emily went down to the lobby newsstand. She bought two newspapers and a magazine.

Before going up to her room she asked if there any messages for her. ButHowever, there was none and quickly she went.Emily then said to Pierre to eat…"Maintenat nous pouvais mange."

Emily poured the coffee meanwhile Pierre buttered the fresh croissants…"Merci Emily."

Quietly they ate their breakfast. Afterwards Pierre left and Emily was alone. He told her he would call her later. Meanwhile she browsed through the newspaper for ads of apartments or rooms for rent. She looked at few she made some circles. She wanted one close to her classes.

She was starting her classes the next day. She had a few preparations to make. She would go buy a few essentials later in the afternoon and at the same time she would look into the addresses.

Moments later the telephone rang. She answered and it was her mother…"Hello Emily. This is your mother. How are you dear?"

Twelve

The evening has just initiated. Pierre asked Emily if she wanted to go for a walk on the Champs-Elysees. He knew she would love to go for café au lait. It sounded all right for her. She had rested a couple hours. They took a taxi, and the driver left them close to the Arc de Triomphe.

Emily's memories came back to her they walked down holding hands. They were esthetic with happiness especially Emily. Then they sat down at one of the side cafés.

Emily had missed all the excitement of being in Paris. It was the beginning of fall, the air began to get chilly. But it was still wonderful to be outside.

Emily spoke to Pierre about her plans and what she done. She told him she was working hard.

As soon her mother left she would begin classes at the American School. She would be taking a course in the fashion houses. It didn't matter at that time what type of a job it would be.

She would make a few applications around the famous houses. She explained to Pierre she hoped something would turn out. Her mother would be staying two weeks in Paris. Pierre listened to all her ideas; he was impressed and at the sametime, happy for her.

She explained that her mother would be staying for two weeks and she would be showing the sights.

After a while Pierre asked Emily if she wanted to spend the night in his apartment. He was missing her so much and needed her. She had a few minutes to think about it then she said for one hour or two the most.

They took a taxi towards the suburbs and a few minutes later. Both were standing waiting for the elevator to come down. These areas were familiar to her she had been there before. Emily walked in.

Pierre knew she couldn't resist his offer. He prepared a very lavish feast for both of them to snack around the late hours of the morning.

The French champagne was chilling in the ice bucket and he had a tray with pastries. Emily sat down on the sofa while he got the champagne, poured the two.

Then they both toasted each…"Pour nous cherie, Emily."

Emily raised the glass and touched his and then said…

"Pour nous vie Pierre."

She slowly sipped her champagne and tasted the delicious pastries. Suddenly Pierre came closer to her his eyes met hers. He embraced her his cheeks touched hers. His lips touched hers and moments later they were both deeply involved with tense feelings. They were once again in love with each other. He went closer and pulled her, in to his arms and carried her across to his bedroom.

He gently let her then they were again embraced and slowly he began to take her clothing. But for a moment Emily got up. She kissed him in his both cheeks…"Pierre mom amour. Je t'aime mais…je suis tres fatique cette nuit."

"Mais Emily…je vous aime ma petite."

Although she had slept a few hours after her arrival she was feeling tired. She didn't also want to leave her mother by herself. There would be a lot of nights, which they could spend together.

She knew if, they would begin something it would last all night.

"Bien Pierre."

After she had spoke those words she realized she had been away from Pierre so long. Maybe she would reconsider what she had to say. She agreed to stay a little longer…"Oui Pierre. Je pouvais etait ici avec vous Pierre."

"Pierre was happy his eyes were lit up with joy…"Bien Emily. Je suis heureux."

After all it didn't make any difference. They went on making love to each other. Quickly they slipped under the white sheets. They felt warm and they touched each other. Pierre knew that Emily was very important to him. There hadn't been another relationship beside Emily.

They stopped for a while then Pierre opened his dressing drawer.

He took a box wrapped with a pretty bow. Then he kissed her and handed it to her. She wasn't expecting that from Pierre. She slowly unwrapped, the box. She saw a beautiful engagement ring. Pierre took the ring and slipped onto her finger. Emily smiled at Pierre and she embraced him. It was a confirmation of their engagement…"Oui Pierre."

Emily smiled as Pierre told her he would take her back to the hotel…"Oui Pierre."

One half an hour later Emily was opening the door of the hotel room. She was a very quiet and she got undressed. Then slipped under the sheets but soon the light of the day came through the window.

Her mother got up and began to get ready for a new day in Paris. Her mother knew it she had come really late.

Minutes later a garcon brought the continental breakfast. Emily's mother opened the door and the garcon left a tray with the breakfast in the coffee table.

She thanked the garcon.

Emily's mother then had her petit-dejeuner by herself.

Finally Emily awoke.

"Good morning mamma." She said to her mother but it was already afternoon.

"Did I sleep all this time?"…Emily paused for a moment…"Mamma you have not eaten yet."

"Emily I had my breakfast hours ago."

"I am relieved. I am sorry about this mamma. Although I have good news."

"What is it?"

"Pierre proposed to me last night. I wasn't expecting it."

"Emily that is good news but have you thought about what are you going to do?"

"Mamma…I still wanted to go in the fashion career. I don't think we are marrying right away. We have still to talk about."

"Why don't you get dressed so we can go for lunch."

"Mamma…I will take a few minutes."

Meanwhile Emily was getting dressed she wondered in her mind a nice place to have lunch and at the same time sightseeing. After a few thoughts something came to her mind: the Bateaux Mouches would be lovely.

They had to rush in order to be able to get there in time. They had to take the metro then go to the Pont de l'Alma.

The weather was cool but it was sunny. It was a nice day for a cruise on the Seine.

Her mother had brought a pocket camera with her. She was wanted a few memories to take back home.

"Are you enjoying the scenery mother?" Emily had seen it all before but it was a nice to see a second time around…"Yes dear."

The lunch wasn't bad at all. They were enjoying the company of each other.

"Emily do you mind taking a photo."

"Smile…mamma would it right there."

The afternoon went in rapidly, they finished the tour. They stepped out from the cruise boat they walked back to the nearest metro. Then they stop at the Opera. They walked back to the hotel where it was already late afternoon.

"Emily are you having dinner with Pierre tonight?"

"I don't know mamma. Maybe he is working he will call."

The evening approached but there was no confirmation about the meeting. It was around seven thirty when the telephone rang.

Emily answered it someone special was in the other end of the line. Pierre called her apologizing about the dinner that they had planned. The reason he had to cancel because he had to work that evening.

"Mamma…Pierre can not make it tonight. So we will have an earlier dinner. I want to go early to bed."

"All right Emily."

They both changed and went down to the restaurant. Two hours later both daughter and mother were back to their room. Emily looked in her brochures about the school. In a few days she would begin her classes. Some of them would be in the morning and the others in the afternoon. She began to apply to the different fashion houses. The next day she would hand in the applications.

Meanwhile her mother had retired for the evening. Emily was looking around for information about apartments or some kind of place so she could move out from the hotel.

Emily for a while she would stay with her mother. Suddenly the telephone rang and she answers it.

"Oui."

"Bon nuit Emily. Comme ca va vous ma cherie?"

"Bien Pierre. Merci."

They spoke for a while on the telephone. Then he suggested they should have an engagement dinner with his parents and her mother. He would make some reservations for dinner at the Lido casino. After they could see a show.

Emily had agreed with Pierre. They would probably choose the follow Saturday.

After all her mother will be leaving in the follow week. They still had a lot to talk about it. Then it was time to say good night. They both said…"Bon nuit."

Emily then went to bed.

When she was awake the next day. They had their breakfast and then made some plans.

"Mamma…how about us taking a tour of the city. There are half day tours of the city or maybe a whole day one."

"It sounds great to me Emily."

"Mamma…I will go down at the desk see if they could make the reservations for us."

Emily came down to the lobby. The receptionist made a few calls.Emily quickly went to her room. Meanwhile they had an hour to get ready and be at the departure area.

Emily hadn't taken the key when she knocked at the door it took a few moments for her to answer. She was in the telephone speaking with her husband.

"Has something happened…mamma?"

"I was speaking to your father. He dialed and he misses us. But I said it won't be too long."

Minutes later they left the hotel they walked towards the metro. They walked towards the metro.

They were lucky they had arrived a few minutes before their departure.

They step inside of the second deck of the charter bus. They sat comfortably and slip the earphones because they could hear the English version. The driver began to move.

They began their tour Emily had been there to the same places. The faces of the crowds were different. No matter how many times you seen these marvelous places there was always a sight.

In one of the stops was the famous Cathedral of Notre Dame. Emily's mother walked in the church towards the front seat and she kneeled. Then prayed for her daughter and her new son in law to be a nice young Frenchman. Then it was the time to walk back to the group.

Emily stood there waiting for her mother to come back. Then a few minutes later she was at her side.

"Are you feeling better mamma."

"Yes I feel much better and after all my soul is more peaceful."

"Mamma it is time to step inside of the bus."

"Let's go in then."

The driver began to move away after checking if all the passengers were in.

Meanwhile they began to speak about their relationship between her and Pierre. Emily still wanted to complete her studies and get a part time job. They spoke a lot of many things. She was being very positive in her thinking.

The morning passed quickly any other one. Then they had a break for lunch. Afterwards they would resume their tour.

They went in one of the small typical French restaurants. Emily orders for her and her mother. They talked for a while and at the same time enjoying each other company.

They were having a good relationship between daughter and mother. They top it out with a French pastry. Then they left they walked towards the bus depot.

One half an hour later they were in the move again. The tour finished in two hours time.

They took the metro again they got out to the nearest stop from the hotel. By then for Emily's knew almost every place.

Emily checked for any messages in the lobby. Yes there was one from Pierre. There was the message to meet him at the lobby at seven o'clock to go out for dinner.

Emily began to get ready for dinner for her mother she would have dinner in by herself in one of the, at the local restaurant.

Emily looked at her wardrobe she found something suitable for the evening. She borrowed her mother pearls for her final touch. A little dab of her perfume in the right places. Then she was ready.

"Emily you looked sensational."

"Thanks mother."

She didn't wait to long for Pierre. Soon the telephone rang. It was he would be waiting for her in the lobby. Moments later she was walking towards the sofa where he was sitting. She smiled and approached him.

"Bon soir Emily. Comme ca va vous?"

"Bien merci."

"Ma cherie vous etes fantastiques…bien."

Pierre led Emily by her hand they walked out to the street. He opened the side door of the brown Porsche. She sat down comfortably while Pierre walked to the other side of the car. He inserted the key in the ignition and drove away. She was impressed of his new car…"Que ce que vous dit sur moi Porsche?"

"Oui bien."

Pierre drove to a narrow street he stopped in the right stop. They got out the car and walked to the tiny and cozy bistro. Then Pierre followed her.

The maitre d' showed to their table. They looked at the menu Pierre suggested to Emily to choose something different.

Pierre chose something French with a bottle of red wine. They made a toast to each other. Emily was very emotional that evening. They had in their mind romance. They had a marvelous dinner and both were very happy. But then it was time to leave she walkedtowalked to the car. Emily laughed with Pierre and he pulled her towards him his lips touched hers and kissed her deeply. A few tears came down her cheeks she was full of joy and her mind was at last rewarded for all the long weeks away from. Suddenly he looked at her face and saw those little tears coming down.

"Que ce que passe ma cherie?" He though it must have been something he did or perhaps something he had said.

He must have offended her.

"Pierre je suis tres heureuse. C'etait ca."

"Oui je comprend ma petite."

After a moment of silence they walked to the car. Somehow that night they should spend with each other. She needed him and his passion but first of the most his understanding.

They stepped inside of the Porsche. Pierre drove away both were silence. He drove around Paris and after minutes of driving he stopped at one of the flower vendors. He stepped out of the car and bought a half an hour dozen of roses.

Quickly he got in he handed her the roses.

"Merci Pierre." Then he drove away. Minutes later he stopped at by his apartment. They took the elevator to his apartment. He opened the door…"Entre Emily." Pierre said to Emily for her to get comfortable. He walked to the kitchen and prepared two glasses with a liqueur. He brought a tray with some French pastries.

Emily sat down in the sofa she was comfortable. Suddenly she got the urge for listening to music. She chose a cassette and inserted into the stereo. Then she sat down. Moments, later Pierre brought the tray. Then he served her and they sat closed to each other. He looked at her eyes. Pierre bent his head; they both touched lips. He went into her.

Their bodies were interlocked with each other and their passion was great.

They were really emotional she said yes. Emily got up from sofa and walked to the bedroom.

She gently took her strapless polka dot dress and slipped into Pierre's brown satin robe. She felt comfortable about it and still he was out there. But Emily somehow felt more relaxed that evening than she felt before

She was very much in love with Pierre. She was glad she had come back to Paris.

Emily lay inside of the warm white sheets she had turned the lights off and only the outside lights remained.

Emily had been going around and she still didn't get used to the new timetable.

She wasn't sleeping in a permanent bed yet soon she was cozy in Pierre's bed she fell asleep.

Pierre was astonished when he walked into his bedroom…"Oh! Mon petit cherie Emily. Vous etes tres fatigue. Je comprend." He tried not to disturb Emily he slept beside her.

Emily soon awakened. When she realized it which, it wasn't any longer dark here the morning had arrived and she turned Pierre wasn't there.

Moments later he came with a tray with le petite de dejeuner with all those delicious croissants.

The smell of the hot café au lait and it was looking very appetizing. She was famished that morning…

"Merci Pierre."

"Bonjour Emily. Comment ca va vous?"

"Bien Pierre."

Pierre bent it over and kissed her. Then he took the tray from her lap. He gently lay on top of her he kissed her with so much passion. They began making love. Emily's began to have butterflies in her stomach. She was nervous. But soon she forgot everything she was in Pierre's arms.After the beautiful morning, Pierre took Emily's back to the hotel. The next time they would see each other would be the something special.

She would go with her mother which to be a very fine occasion they would meet his parents.

Afterwards her mother would be leaving. She really wanted her father to be there. But of course it was impossible. But for her wedding he said he would be with his daughter.

"Good morning mother." Emily greed her mother.

"Good morning Emily. I see a beautiful smile on your face."

"Mamma I am very happy. I am glad that I met Pierre. We are so much in love."

"Emily at first I thought you had made a big mistake. But now I see you are right. He is a nice young man. He is very gentle. He cares for you."

"Thanks mamma for seeing what I said before."

Her mother hugged her…"Good."

"How about calling your father to tell him about the dinner. Then we should go shopping for that event."

"Yes mamma."

They made the call her father was working at his office. He was glad that they both were together and about the good news.

He wished the time would past fast so he could see his wife. They said their good byes and both the daughter and mother went shopping.

After a long day walking around the small boutiques around Paris. They had arrived by the taxi with their hands full of packages. The porter opened the door and helped with the extra packages…

"Merci."

They went up to their room.

"Mamma I am famished how about putting all these away and go out for dinner just the two of us."

"Right Emily."

A half an hour later they both were ready. They walked down to the lobby. Emily went to the reception desk and asked about information about a restaurant for them to go.

Emily went to go and she wrote down the name in the piece of paper. Then they both walked outside. Then called out for a taxi…"Merci."

Minutes later the driver left them at the front of the restaurant. There was no reservation but the maitre d' lead them to the table. It had turned into a nice evening.

Emily talked with her mother and about her plans. But there was no plan in any wedding or anything. They were just engaged at that point. Emily still wanted to go in with her career after the departure of her mother. She would begin her classes and then she had to look for a part time job.

She had already a few things so she could begin to sketch her own designs. It would take probably a long way for her to get anywhere. But she didn't mind it all. She had to start some where.

The follow week she would begin her first classes and she looked for it. Her dreamed was to become one day a designer. But it was a still a long way out and all of those ideas she had spoke to her mother.

Her mother listened to her very attentive both seemed to be enjoying their mother and daughter relationship.

They finished their dinner and they left.

"Let's see if we can find a taxi."

Emily and her mother walked up to the street there was only a small crowd, Besides it was a pleasant walk the cafes were always crowded.

"Mamma would you mind if we stopped for a café au lait anyway it isn't to late and night enjoy ourselves. Soon mamma you will be going back to the winter and it will be a long season."

"I won't mind at all Emily."

Moments later they both sat down at the tiny round table.

Both were happy after a few moments the garcon approached the table…"Oui Mademoiselle."

"Deux cafes au lait s'il vous plait."

"Bien."

"Mamma do you miss dad?"

"Yes but I am used to it. Sometimes your father goes away a day or two. But…anyway I will go home soon."

"I will try to be in touch."

Moments later the garcon brought the two cafes au lait.

"Merci"

Emily opened the tiny package of sugar slip a little bit in the white coffee to sweeten it…"This tastes good mamma."

"They really know how to make a good cup of coffee and quite different from back home." "Yes mamma."

"So in two days we will meet Pierre's parents."

"I am a bit nervous but it will be all right."

"I will be here for any moral support if you need it."

"Thanks mamma. I will appreciated very much."

They sat there for a little while longer then it was time to leave.
"Mamma should we leave?"
"Yes dear. It is getting late."
Emily called the garcon paid. Then both left the café Emily signal for a taxi. Then she was lucky she got one. She had the driver to drive them to the hotel.

Thirteen

Later Emily tried to be in touch with Pierre. But he hadn't arrived at his apartment.

She decided to call him the next day. Then she was going to bed. She lay in the bed for a while before falling turning in. She had a lot of thinking to do.

"Good night mamma."

"Good night Emily."

Emily lay awake in the dark, which was a transaction time for her. She knows for sure there are a lot of work to do. She would get something back in return she was happy. The city was great to be living in which she had aspirations and she had found her love. It seemed that everything was turning out all night.

That day was a gray autumn one her mother got up early and ordered room service. She got up and took a shower by the time she got out from the bathroom. The breakfast was set in the table near the window.

"This smells good mamma…I see there is a fresh pot of coffee."
"Let's eat now before everything gets cold."

"All right mamma. But I am not dress yet."

"It is okay Emily."

The two of them had a leisure breakfast. The day was going to be a really fall day which she had to plan for the day. Maybe it was a nice day to spend in the museum. There was something she had to do

Before going to it. She had to made applications for a part time job.

"Mamma this breakfast tasted well. I guess my stomach was empty."

"I am glad you had enjoy."

"I am getting dressed now so I can go out for a little while. Before we would spend a few hours in the Louvre. It is a nice day to spend inside."

Emily looked into the closet and she took out something suitable to look for a job.

"Yes she thought this will fit well her brown suit. She took it from the closet with her brown shoes with the matching bag.

An hour later she was all set to go…"See you later mamma. I will back around two hours time."

"Good luck Emily." Her mother told her she hoped her daughter would fine something.

Emily walked to the nearest metro.

Soon she got in the metro towards one of the experience streets of Paris. She took time in the Avenue Montaigne, there was the Christian Dior house and many more such, Guy Laroche Nina Ricci. After going through all of these places. She was amazed she applied for anything it didn't matter. All of them answered the same answer. But she went to other famous houses and other small boutiques around.

Even she went into the some of the elegant department stores. She walked into the Galeries Lafayette.

She went into the main office and left her application. She decided that was it. In the Galeries of Lafatette in the main floor she walked to the cosmetic area and bought a small bottle of her favorite French perfume.

Meanwhile she decided to a break in one of the outside cafes close by. She sat at one of the empty tables she took out her small notebook. She made notes of all the places she had been.

"Oui Mademoiselle." "A café au lait et un perrier s'il vous plait."

"Oui Mademoiselle."

Moments later the garcon brought in a round tray a bottle of cool mineral water and a white cup of coffee. Emily thanked the garcon…"Merci."

"Oui Mademoiselle."

The weather for an instant it seemed to change to a cool and windy. She was warmed dressed but she felt too chilly to be outside to long. She finished her coffee and thought that the few days her mother would be leaving Paris. She looked at her watch she saw it was time for her to move in. She called the garcon to pay.

An hour later she was knocking at the door of the hotel room. It takes a few minutes before her mother answering.

"Is that you Emily?" Her mother spoke out loud.

"Yes mamma." Emily answered back and her mother opened the door…."How is your search coming along?"

"Mamma…time will tell and I hope I can be accepted in one of them. I made several application."

"Emily don't worried for now."

"Mamma what are we going to do this afternoon?"

"How about we going to the Louvre. I need to freshen up a bit."

"All right I will get ready."

In half an hour both mother and daughter were set to leave the hotel room. They took the elevator to the lobby. Then they walked out to the street.

"Is a bit chilly today. How about us taking a taxi to the nearest metro?" "Mamma…I don't mind at all. The weather is all right we will get used from back home." "Then we will take a taxi and it's my treat." "Right"…Then the porter called out a taxi. Then they step inside.

The taxi driver stopped at the Rue de Rivoli. They walked a few stairs they bought the tickets to get in.

Moments later, they both were walking through the corridors of the Louvre. There were some spots more crowded than others. They walked and looked stopped at the famous works of art. They looked into the Renaissance period in history. They stayed at certain periods in history longer than the other they both appreciated the knowledge of art culture. After looking at art and they took a break in which they walked out for lunch.

After a French lunch they went back to the Orangerie des Tulleries they looked at the of the Monet famous painting wall the Waterlilies.

Both mother and daughter were very much impressed at the marvelous painting of the lilies. Emily had seen it when she was in Paris.

After a while in the lovely time spend in the marvelous places and it was time to leave. They take the metro at Concord.

Emily's mother was really happy being with her daughter in Paris. Besides that was a change to know each other better.

They were sitting down and talked they promised to be in touched by writing. Emily wanted very much for her father to meet Pierre maybe in the following spring or summer.

Meanwhile they arrived at Madeleine stop. They walked towards the hotel Seze. There was one message from Pierre…."He will meet her around seven thirty at the lobby and for them to go out for dinner."…Emily was delightful with the written note.

Emily quickly changed her clothing for an evening out. Soon she was back in the lobby. She sat down and wondered away. Pierre was a little bit late.

Finally she saw him coming. She got up and went to meet him. She smiled at himandhim and she embraced, then, she kissed him .

He showed her a lot of affection each time they saw each other. There was lot, times, she was a bit reserved towards him.

"Bon soir ma Cherie Emily."

"Bon soir Pierre."

Pierre takes Emily's hand they walked out to the car. He decided to go somewhere special for dinner. He looked at her she was looking very attractive. He didn't spoke where they would be going. He was happy with Emily. They both were enjoying each other's company.

Emily spoke to Pierre about her plans. Her various applications for a few any kind of job. She told him she had applied in different places. On a few days she will be starting her classes.

He looked so elegant and well manner. She couldn't resist his baby blue eyes so his rosy white face.

He was a very attractive in that way to her.

They were approaching a closed by a huge sign. At that moment she knows where she was going too.

Pierre parked his Porsche near by then they walked to the restaurant. "Le voila Emily."

Emily smiled at him they held their hands…"Oui Pierre."

What a wonderful evening they both had. Pierre brought her back to the hotel. They stood inside they kissed deeply until it was time to say good night. She had to rest so she was meeting his parents for the first time.

It was important to her to make a good impression. They will be having a elegant dinner. She was little bit nervous because she had no idea what to expect.

"Bon nuit Pierre."

Pierre drove away, she stepped inside of the lobby of the hotel.

Quickly she went to her room and opened the door. Her mother was in a deep sleep. Soon she waas in bed too. Moments later she was asleep.

Finally it came the moment so they would meet his parents late afternoon. Emily was dressed elegantly and so was her mother. Pierre came to get them at the hotel. His parents were waiting at the casino for a memorable evening.

Pierre let them at the main entrance of the Lido. Minutes, later Pierre came in and looked for the two of them. Meanwhile Emily seemed to be a bit nervous her mother told her it was going to be fine.

Pierre approached his parents whom where just outside of the restaurant. First Pierre greeted his parents since he hadn't seen them for a little while. Then he held Emily's hand. He spoke to his father and mother he introduced Emily and her mother…"It is a pleasure to meet you Madame…MomsieurMonsieur…"

"Enchante Emily."

"Madame Simpsone."

"Enchante Madame."

They talked for a little while until it was time to talk to the restaurant. The maitre d' showed the reserved table. Pierre's mother seemed to get along with Emily.

They spoke to each other for a while even Pierre's mother offered any support if needed it.

Emily knew soon, she would be alone in a different country. Emily gladly accepted Pierre's mother help.

At the end of the meal, Pierre ordered a bottle of French champagne, they toasted the young couple.

"To Pierre and Emily engagement."

"Pierre…Emily."

They finished saluting each other, Emily sipped the champagne in the flute glass at the same time smiling at Pierre. Then his eyes looked at her, he was wishing to touch her. Both got their signs across and Emily excused herself to the ladies room she gets up. Pierre also got up.

"Excuse-moi"

Moments later both bumped into each other and Pierre couldn't resist her any longer "Oui Emily."

"Oui Pierre vous aime."

"Oui ma Cherie Emily."

They couldn't help each other. Pierre takes Emily he held her closer to him. He kissed her deeply just where they were. After a while both of them felt very good.

Afterwards they went back where their parents were. They sat down at the table…"Emily ca va bien?

Et vous mon chere Pierre."

"Oui ma mere."

Everyone soon walked out the evening show was about to begin. Pierre held Emily's hand tightly.

Maybe they will be spending the evening together. But Emily would stay with her mother she would be leaving soon. After the show each said their good bye and then left.

Pierre takes Emily and her mother she would be leaving soon. After the show each said their good byes and then they left.

Pierre takes Emily and her mother back to the hotel. Upon the arrival at the hotel her mother went right away to her room. Meanwhile Emily stayed a little longer with Pierre.

The night has been very successful with each other future in laws. Pierre held Emily in his arms they kissed. Emily heart began to beat faster. Maybe in the following weeks they wouldn't be able to see each other much.

Then it was time to leave Pierre takes Emily up to her room. They kissed they touched each other until the door open. A few steps Emily was in front of the door.

"Bon nuit." Pierre said good night and then left, he turned around and blew a kiss, he waved.

Emily slowly opened the door and closed it. Her mother was already asleep.

Emily quickly turned in.

She was tired and the night had turned well after all she was any longer nervous. Finally it came the day for Emily's mother to leave Paris.

"Good morning mamma. How are you feeling this morning?"

Emily wondered if her mother were feeling uneasy to be leaving her. But it turned out not to be so she knew it she would be capable of handling herself properly.

"Emily how about having a lavish breakfast."

"Mamma that is a good idea. "

Her mother and daughter got ready to go out. Emily had enough time to spend with her mother. The flight from Paris to Toronto would be leaving in the late hours of the evening. It had been wonderful for both of them.

They both had a chance to know each other differently not just mother and daughter but a friend.

"Mamma are you ready?" Emily picked her winter coat it was chilly outside her mother was ready to leave.

"Yes dear. Let me pick up the French scarf."

Moments later both walked out from the hotel. The restaurant was just near by in a narrow street. The two entered the restaurants the fresh smell of French coffee.

They were hungry just from the fresh smell of baking goods. They sat at in one of the empty table. Moments later the garcon brought the two menus. Emily browsed and right away she chose and at the same time asks what her mother wanted. The garcon came back to the table.

"Oui Mademoiselle…Madame…Bien vous etes pretes?"

"Pour nous deux croissants avec beurre et café au lait s'il vous plait."

"Merci."

"Emily are you going to look for an apartment?"

"Yes mamma. I have too it won't be too easy. I would like some place close by the school."

"I am sure you will find some place. Maybe Pierre can help you. Remember he knows the city or any connections that he has."

"I have been looking in the newspapers and any place have passed by. This is a nice place. Maybe Pierre can help. Remember he knows the city or any connections that he has."

"I have been looking in the newspaper and any place have passed by. This is a nice place have passed by. This is a nice place it will turned to be too much for me."

"Do you need any money Emily?"

"I am all right for now mamma."

The garcon brought then the fresh continental breakfast…"Merci."

"These croissants are really fresh Emily."

"I have been here before and the food tastes good and very afford-able. I really like these croissants and they taste the best of all of them."

They finished their breakfast. There was still time they could spend talking. Emily asked the garcon for deux café au lait. Some how the sun appeared again and the day seemed to be brighter.

Finally it was time to leave and Emily's mother paid. Then they walked out they walked towards the hotel there were a few little shops in the way.

Emily's mother suggested walking in in one of the very elegant boutique.

"Let's go in Emily. I like to browse in. Maybe I will find something for me."

The clothes were very distinguished French and all the accessories.

"Mamma this handbag is beautiful."

"Emily be free to look around if you see something. I will buy it a good bye present."

Her mother saw something else she liked and bought it. Then they left. But near the hotel there was a small men shop. Emily's mother went in to buy something for her husband. She then bought a silky tie.

Then minutes later they were at the lobby of the hotel. There was a message from Pierre. He asking what time was her mother's flight. He left the telephone number where he can be reached. They went up to the room.

Her mother finished packing then Emily called Pierre. He told her for them to be in the lobby at seven thirty because the flight was at nine thirty.

Fourteen

There was plenty time before the flight. Emily decided it was a good time for lunch and a little bit of sightseeing. She would do both at the same time and the place for that was the Eiffel Tower.

"It is fine with me Emily."

They took the metro to the nearest stop, which was Champ de Mars Tour Eiffel. Afterwards they would take the elevator to the right floor.

The maitre d' showed their table they sat a good table. Meanwhile Emily looked at the menu she chose something for her and her mother.

Finally it came the day for Emily's mother to leave Paris.

"Good morning mamma. How are you feeling uneasy to be leaving her but it turned out not to be so she knew it she would be capable of handling herself properly."

"Emily how about having a lavish breakfast."

"Mamma that is a good idea. There is a small restaurant close by. We can finish packing."

"Yes Emily. It is a wonderful idea."

Her mother and daughter got ready to go out. Emily had enough time to spend with her mother. The flight from Paris to Toronto would be leaving in the later hours of the evening in the late hours of the evening. It had been wonderful for both of them.

They both had a chance to know each other differently not just a mother and daughter but a friend.

"Mamma are you ready?" Emily picked her winter coat it was chilly outside her mother was ready to leave.

"Yes dear. Let me picked up the French scarf."

Moments later both walked out from the hotel. The restaurant was just near by in a narrow street.

The two entered the restaurant there it was a fresh aroma of French coffee.

They sat at in one of the empty tables. Moments later the garcon hand out two menus. Emily browsed through it and asked what her mother wanted. The garcon came back to the table.

"Oui Mademoiselle…Madame…Bien vous etes pretes?"

"Pour nous deux croissants avec beurre et café au lait s'il vous plait."

"Merci"

"Emily are you going to look for an apartment?"

"Yes mamma. I have too it won't be too easy. I would like some place. Maybe Pierre can help you. Remember he knows the city or any connections that he has."

"I have been looking in the newspapers and any place have passed by. This is a nice place it will turned to be too much for me."

"Do you need any money Emily."

"I am all right for now mamma."

The garcon brought them the fresh continental breakfast…

"Merci."

"These croissants are really fresh Emily?"

"I have been here before and the food tastes good and very affordable. I really like these croissants and they taste the best of all them."

They finished their breakfast. There was still time they could spend talking. Emily asked the garcon for deux café au lait. Some how the sun appeared again and the day seemed to be brighter. Finally it was time to leave and Emily's mother paid. Then they walked out towards the hotel. There were a few shops in between. Emily's mother, suggest walking in one of the elegant ones. The clothes were very distinguished French and all the accessories.

"Mamma this handbag is beautiful."

"Emily be free to look by present."

Her mother saw something else she liked and bought it. Then they left. But near the hotel there was a small men shop. Emily's mother went in to buy something for her husband. She then bought a silky tie.

Then minutes later they were at the lobby of the hotel. There was a message from Pierre. He was asking what time was her mother's flight. He left the telephone number where he can be reached. They

Went up to the room.

"Mamma…how do you like the view?" Emily had been there before she wondered if her mother had been there too.

"Emily is a nice view from up here the city had a very different prospect from an higher view."

There were so many different historic monuments.

"Yes you are right mamma."

Her mother takes her pocket camera to take a few photos. The garcon was passing by Emily asked politely for him to take a photo at them.

"Merci."

Then moments later the waiter approached their table…

"Vous avez choisi Madame…Mademoiselle."

"Oui." She responded with a yes.

"Bien…La salade russe et le bouef a la mode. C' est ca pour nous deux."

"Merci."

Emily turned to her mother then asked if she wanted wine or any other beverage.

"All right Emily. We shall have red wine then."

Later the wine waiter came to the table. She spoke in French they had chosen the wine…"Oui Mademoiselle."

"Emily those past two weeks have been a real joy for me. I hope Emily everything will go well with you. Maybe I can convince your father to come to Paris even if it is just for a week or less."

"Mamma that is a good idea maybe by spring time will come to visit all of you. Since it is so much beautiful around the month of May."

The waiter brought the wine he showed to Emily and she said…"Oui. C'est ca…"

He opened the bottle and poured into Emily's glass then to her mother.

"Let's make a toast." Her mother lift, the glass towards Emily…"To you and Pierre."

"I will drink to that mamma…thank you."

Minutes later the waiter brought the salads and the main course…"How is it?" Emily asked her mother…"It tastes good."

After a delicious meal both had same dessert. Emily chose mousse au chocolate. Her mother had a French pastry.

"C' estest. ca?" The waiter came to the table and asked if everything was all right.

"Oui…deux café au lait s' il vous plait."

"Oui Mademoiselle."

Emily finished her wine while waiting for her coffee.

"So mamma…do you want to go anywhere else? We will have two hours before going leaving to the airport."

"No…we are going back to the hotel."

"All right mamma."

They relaxed a little bit longer while they sipped their coffee. After a long while the waiter brought the bill.

But it was her mother's treat.

"Merci." The two were walking towards the metro. One half an hour later they were walking into the lobby. Emily checked for any messages but there was one message from Pierre. It saidhesaid he would be there in one hour or less…

Emily and her mother went up to their room. Emily's mother was all packed and she only needed to rearrange her handbag with her personal belongings. She takes her luggage and left at the door.

Emily came down to get a newspaper she was looking in the ads for a place to move in. She could stay in one more week in the hotel. Then she would leave otherwise she had that expense.

She had not yet any answers for her part time applications she hoped to hear something soon. Her classes would begin in two days.

Meanwhile her mother made a telephone call to her husband. It took a matter of a few minutes. On the other side of the world it was earlier in the morning.

Emily spoke a few words she said hello to her father. Then she passed the telephone to her mother she spoke to him only a few minutes. She would see him in a few hours. He wished her a safe trip and would see her in a couple hours.

"Mamma do you want a tea with a biscuit before Pierre gets here?"

"Emily that is a excellence idea."

Emily called the desk a few minutes later the garcon came with a tray with their good byes. Moments later the garcon knocked at the door.

Emily opened the door she signed the bill and tipped the garcon.

"Merci Mademoiselle."

Both mother and daughter sat by the round table by the window. They enjoyed the cup of tea and the last few words before leaving. Then fifteen minutes later afternoon break.

"Oui" She said out loud…"Pierre." He answered back. Emily opened the door and Pierre kissed her he came into the room. He agreed his mother in law to be.

Her mother was ready to leave. But she had left she went to the reception desk to pay the bill.

She paid also an extra week for her daughter to stay in. At least Emily didn't have to worry for a week. Soon she came up to the room. Meanwhile Pierre was deeply kissing Emily and both were in touch with each other.

"Ma Cherie Emily…ma amour." In that moment there was a knocked at the door. They came apart and composed themselves.

"Emily everything is paid and I also left a week for you to stay."

"Thanks mamma. You shouldn't have."

"It is all right dear."

Her mother then went to use the bathroom to touch up a bit before leaving.

"Excuse me for a moment."

Then Emily picked her coat and called the porter to come up to get her mothers baggage.

Moments later the porter was knocking at the door. Emily opened and he picked the baggage and left. Afterwards Emily's opened came out she was ready to leave for the airport.

"Emily it is time to leave."

"Right mamma." Emily spoke to Pierre that it was time for them to leave. A few minutes later they all left and Emily's mother sat in the back of the car. Emily sat beside Pierre they talked to each other.

Upon the arrival at the Gaille Airport Pierre got out of the car and takes the luggage out from the trunk. Then all they walked inside towards the airline counter. Emily's mother checked in.

They had an hour to be with each other before the departure time.

Later they said theirs good byes to each other. Emily embraced her mother it was a very emotional.

Then she walked to the departure area. Emily's mother waved back to her. Then they stayed there until her mother had gone.

Pierre and Emily walked to the car. He drove away it was early in the evening. It was time for dinner he asked her if she was feeling up to have something to eat.

"Oui Pierre." He drove around a bit then he stepped by a bistro. They walked in, The maitre d' showed a cozy table in one of the booths. A bottle of red wine with a French dinner they had a pleasant conversation. They were enjoying their dinner afterwards he takes Emily back to the hotel.

Emily got the key at the reception desk then both went up. They were alone at last. Pierre smiled at Emily he got closer. Her heart began to beat faster and they got very physical. He touched her so close. Then deeply he kissed her. They were making passionate love. Pierre began gently undressing Emily.

The desire became greater each moment passed by. She could feel his power and at the same time his gentleness. He knew what she desired there was so much friction between the two of them. Emily wanted more and more. Soon they had to come up for fresh air…"Oui ma Cherie."

"Pierre…je t'aime."

"Oui…Je t'aime aussi ma belle Emily."

Pierre asked Emily if she wanted to eat or drink something. He called the reception for a bottle of champagne and some fresh strawberries. The receptionist said it was a bit late and it would take longer than any other time.

Pierre said it was allrightall right it didn't matter how long. Almost an hour later there was a knock at the door. Pierre takes the tray from the garcon. He left the tray at the table and takes some money and tipped the busboy.

"Merci Monsieur. Bon nuit."

"Merci."

Pierre closed the door and walked towards Emily. He gentle awakened her. Since she wasn't really asleep but resting…"Oui…Oui."

Pierre takes the cork from the bottle of champagne. Then poured the bubbly into the two tall glasses. Emily sat up with the white sheet wrapped underneath her arms. He handed her the glass they sipped the champagne and ate at the same time the fresh strawberries.

After a while Pierre called Emily to come to him. Emily was closer to him and she kissed him gently in his lips. They embraced him she could smell his masculine scent. She had a tingling feeling.

She kissed him again. He lay down in top of her. Pierre reached the switch and turned the light off.

The phone rang. Emily answered.

"I am fine mamma. Thank you for calling. Did you have a good flight?"

"There was a bit of shaking but I arrived safe. Your father sends love to you. He isn't here right now. I wanted just to talk."

"Thanks for calling mamma. I am well and I was about to leave for an hour or so."

"All right Emily. Good bye for now."

"Good bye mamma. Give my love to father."

Emily put the receiver down.

Later, Emily kept looking at the newspaper. Finally she found a small apartment in the right area she was looking for. To here it was a telephone number she dialed. But there was no answer she would try it again.

She changed her clothing for something more casual. Then wrote down all the addresses in her notebook. Then she should tried to dial that number again. But there was a answer that time…"Oui…oui. C' est. le numero…"

She spoke to a woman. She had convinced her and the price right. She told the woman she would take the place and would move be passing there…"Oui Mademoiselle. Bien je suis ici."

Emily was then relaxed there was one more thing needed which it was to find a job.

But she had to check the place yet. After speaking to this woman. She felt a better because it sounded to be a good place for now. Then she felt the hotel towards the metro. On her list there was a couple things to do. She stopped at one of the French bookshop, which needed a lot of the essentials.

Pencils, drawing paper and a few books. After a few minutes later she had seemed to have enough to carry. She thought that was enough for a while…

"Merci Mademoiselle."

Emily smiled and left. He was a nice man. Who took the time to helped, her told him she had other places to be. Then he said if she needed anything else next time. He would gladly help her.

When she arrived at the hotel there was Pierre waiting for me. She told him she had another

Place to visit. Then they set a time to meet for dinner. He knew from then in. There was no much time they will spend with each other. She was beginning her classes the follow day.

"Au revoir Pierre."

Pierre left Emily went up to the room. She began freshen up a bit then she came down again. Then she left. Emily takes the metro in the direction to the apartment. But she was looking for the location she couldn't find it. Then she was looking at the map someone approached her. He wondered right away if she was a foreigner. He spoke French then it he tried to speak in English. He had congratulated her by speaking French. Then she asked him if he knew where that school was.

He told her it was in the Latin Quarter, he began to introduce himself. She knew right away he was older than Pierre he seemed to know the area very welled, her thought was that he must be an older student or a teacher.

"Je m'appelle Francois de Gouille."

"Bien je m'appelle Emily Jonshon."

"Enchante Mademoiselle."

"C'etait un plaisir Monsieur."

"I am a teacher in the fashion design and the arts."

She was surprised when he spoke about the school. She was glad she had found a friend.

"So you speak English."

"Yes I do."

They began the conversation she told him what she had chosen. A designer the school had been famous for. He told her that she was in good hands. But he wasn't her teacher. She was taking other subjects. She said she was looking for a part-time job so she could support herself. She had applied at different places. They went inside at the school he showed her the classes. There wasn't staff around just the caretakers.

They were preparing the school for the next day. She was happy she had run into Francois. He offered a dinner date with her she had to say no.

"She had an engagement…"Maybe some other time."

"Right Emily."

After a while she left and thanked him for helping her. It made the day easier she the metro to locate the room for rent. It was in a different arrodissement. She looked around and all the area, there was all these typical French houses. She had the sign for rent. She rang the doorbell a few times. She waited a little while until she heard some footsteps closing by. A woman around of a middle age opened the door and then said…"Oui Mademoiselle."

"Je m'appelle Emily. Je viens ici pour voir votre."

"Bien bien…entre Mademoiselle."

She followed the woman she was right she was an older woman very close to the fifties. She walked behind her by the staircase. There were a lot of the steps to the third floor and then she opened a door. At first sight it looked all right. The small window had a view looking a small park. The bed was small and a smaller dresser with the mirror in front. But the bathroom was downstairs in the second floor. Emily didn't say much just smiled at the woman. She seemed to be speaking too much. Then she said the amount for the room but Emily wanted to find out something different. She told the woman she would give an answer by the end of the week.

"Oui Mademoiselle."

"Au revoir Madame."

The French woman closed the door after Emily and then waved back to her. In the meanwhile,

Emily had to see if she could find something else. But if there was no other place she had no choice than to take it.

She had a few more days until she commit herself she passed by a magazine stand and bought a newspaper maybe that that time she could fine what she was looking for. But it was getting late the time approaching for her to meet Pierre for dinner. She had still to change her clothing.

She was walking inside of the hotel. She looked around to see if Pierre was around. But he wasn't she felt much relief. Quickly she went up to her room. She takes a dressed and then came down to the lobby. She sat down she waited for him. The time passed and he didn't showed up. She began to worry.

Meanwhile Emily was getting hungry. She hadn't eaten much but her mind was a lot of thoughts some were good and others aren't. Then out of the blue he walked in. Immediately he saw her.

"Perdon moi Emily."

"Bien Pierre. Nous allons."

"Oui ma Cherie."

They walked out she stepped inside of his car. Moments later he drove away. She was silent. He didn't spoke either. She wasn't mad at him simply feeling her empty stomach. He felt that was something wrong. It couldn't have been showing up late. Pierre takes only fifteen minutes to arrive at the restaurants he had made reservations earlier. After they had chosen what they wanted to eat. The main course was served and towards the end Emily felt better. Her stomach was full. Afterwards she told about what kind of a day she had.

"Oui Emily." He said holding her hands gently squeezing and at the same time smiling to her.

Pierre asked her if she was nervous about her classes…"Je suis bien."

She told him from that point in it would be different to see him as much as she could.

"Je comprend Emily."

She told him about meeting Francois. He was glad for her having there someone if she needed. The dinner was coming to an end by that time it was getting late. Both agree to leave Emily had morning classes next day.

Later they arrived at the hotel. They say good night and Pierre kissed Emily deeply they hugged and said...

"Bon nuit."

Pierre left. Emily went up to the room she was tired from a busy night. Quickly she got ready to bed.

Moments, later Emily fell asleep.

The new morning began for Emily. She got up before seven o'clock, as was going to be busy day. Just as eight o'clock turned she left the hotel towards the metro. She hadn't ate as, she went underground and she bought a café au lait with two croissants in one of the coffees shops. She watched the crowds going by it was rush hour.

She held her briefcase and her shoulder bag she was in the way to her classes. Emily arrived at the school twenty minutes before her first class. The first person she saw was Francois. He was checking some papers for his students and holding his schedule.

"Bonjour Emily. How are you?"

"Bonjour Professeur Francois Plantee. This morning I feel a little bit nervous." "You will be all right...Emily if you need anything just ask the secretary to call."

Afterwards Emily left. She had located the room; her first lesson was a fashion sketching which it was one of she would like.

The teacher got acquainted with the twenty students. Emily made friends with some of her colleges. There were some younger her some oldest she would be acquainted with them.

All the morning she had classes then it was time for lunch. Before entering the school area she had passed by small restaurants which were frequentedrestaurants, which were frequented, from the staff and the students from the school. She had to watch her cash flow she wanted to find the job she needed.

On the way to the restaurant she bought the French newspaper. Then walked in and sat in one of the tables. She was looking over the menu. She though of one French country soup and a ham sandwich and half of the baguette would fulfill her. She saw one of the girls coming towards her table.

"Emily est-ce que je pouvais." Helene asked her if she could sit with her. Right way before she finished her sentence she said yes.

"Oui Helene. S' il vous plait."

"Emily…I do speak a little English."

"All right Helene."

Meanwhile the garcon brought her hot soup. Helene looked at Emily's soup. Then she had decided to have the same. The two of them began to talk and began knowing each other better. Then Emily finished her lunch she asked for a café au lait. Emily sipped her café au lait and at the same time browsed through the newspaper.

"Qu' est-ce que vous voir?" Helene asks Emily what she was looking for. She answers her back.

"Ma mere avait une chambre."

"Bien Helene. Est-ce que vous savez combien cette chambre?"

"Non." Helene didn't know how much her mother wanted for the room. But she was going to ask to her. Helene didn't lived far away. Maybe it was perfect Emily, thought about it, then she was to see

it, to make sure if it was right.

Then the two of them went back to the school for the afternoon classes. Time passed quickly and they finished the school for that and everyone went into different directions. Emily said au revoir. She walked back to the metro.

After she had arrived at the hotel then checked the reception desk to see if there was anything for her. But there was no answer from her applications. She would wait for another two days before looking for any other places.

Meanwhile she had some homework to do she sat by the window. She began her work at least was simple at the beginning it would get harder later in for sure. She knew that is always the case.

The winter season was approaching the days began to get shorter. By the time she finished her sketches and her writing work it was dark outside. Then she changed her clothing then went out for dinner.

By then she was exhausted and went to bed.

The next day was worst than the day before. She didn't feel like getting up but she had to it. Already she was running late that morning. She slipped into her casual pants and a wool sweater at least she felt warm inside. She picked up her books and went out to the metro for her classes. She made only a stop to buy a croissant and left. Quickly she went walked to the school and made in time.

She sat down at her desk she smiled at Helene but that morning the schedule was different. The lunchtime came and Emily wanted to know if Helene had any news for her. Both of them went to the same place for lunch.

After all she had good news. Since Emily was in the same school and a friend of her daughter. Her mother made a special price for her. Emily was glad and accepted without seeing the place. She said she would be moving by the beginning of the follow week. In the other hand Emily told her about the new job in the small shop it was close to the hotel where she was staying.

But it didn't matter if she had too travel a bit longer for her job.

"Bien Emily qu' est que vous avez aujourd' hui?" Helene asked what she wanted for lunch.

"Je veux la salade Francaise avec la soupe de jour."

"Je choisi le meme."

They ate and they both left. When the classes ended Emily immediately left and walked towards the metro to the shop. Upon her arrival there was one customer trying some outfit and the owner was tidying up the shelves.

"Bonsoir Madame. Je m'appelle Emily."

"Oh…Oui."

Madame knew right away who she was. She asked if she could start working in a day or two.

"Oui Madame…Demain."

"Bien Emily."

Emily walked out. She went back to the hotel her arms of books. It was late in the afternoon she arrived at the hotel and checked for any messages. But there was none. When she got to her room she decided to rest for a little while because she was tired.

She lay there in bed she had sat the alarm clock for an hour. She had drowned the curtains and Emily fell asleep.

An hour passed the alarm clock went in. It rang a few times before Emily turned it off. But she was too tired to get up. Although it was already early in the evening and she hadn't eaten anything else since lunch. She forced herself up and walked to the bathroom. She washes her face with cold water then she was awake. She picked her coat and handbag and left the room.

She walked towards a narrow street then she went to a bistro. But it was full at that point in the evening. She had to wait for a table. She was famished and she decided to pick something light. In that way she wouldn't take to long.

Finally the maitre d' came back…"Bien Mademoiselle viens avec moi s'il vous plait."

He then handed her a menu…"Merci."

Emily looked, and right away she knew what she wanted. She chose a salad and omelet. When the waiter approached the table she told him what she wanted…"Merci Mademoiselle."

It was a simple request and it didn't take long. After her dinner she left right away. She returned to the hotel and went straight to bed. Soon she fell asleep her body had given up all her strength.

Emily had to know the surroundings until the Madame would leave in her own. It would take her probably a week. Before she was able to be in her own.

Emily had to do her schoolwork upon arrival at the hotel. Madame showed Emily where everything was and she would learn each a little bit. The usual customers walked in Madame asked Emily if she had work in any clothing shop. She responded by a positive answer to Madame.

The last customer left for the evening and it was time to close. It seemed that Madame was pleased with her.

Emily finished arranging everything back to their places. Madame turned the last light of the boutique and at the same time Emily walked outside and then said…

"Bonsoir Mademoiselle. Demain a la meme heure."

"Oui Madame…au revoir."

Emily walked to the metro already was dark. But she wasn't afraid. There was always a crowd around anything of the day and the night. For her dinner she had a quick French ham sandwich in one of the coffee bar closed by.

When she arrived at the hotel she wanted to go up. But the receptionist saw her walking by. Then she called out loud…" Mademoiselle…Mademoiselle." Emily looked back and walked to the desk.

"Bonsoir Mademoiselle. Vous avez une." The receptionist handed out a folded piece of paper.

"Merci." Then she went up to her room. She knew it that the message had to be from Pierre.

She began reading the note she was surprised because it was in English.

"Ma chere Emily. I wonder how are you been I hope all you classes are coming along well. I will be waiting for the telephone call tonight before you go to bed. Adieu Pierre."

It made everything turned all right although she was about to go to bed. It had been an active day.

Meanwhile she was getting ready to sleep but not quiet because she was waiting for Pierre's telephone call.

She had to do some sketches and some reading. Besides her work she wanted to start a spring fashion collection. She would start later in when settling in. She finished her work and she was reading the book in costumes. She was about to turn the third page when the telephone rang. It was Pierre in the other end.

"Bon nuit Emily." They talked for a little while then Emily said to him. She had a place to move. He asked if she was free to go out in the follow Saturday. She was working until six o'clock in the afternoon then each other said good night.

She was working until six o'clock in the afternoon then each other good night.

She finished reading the pages she had too. Then she left the rest for the next day she was exhausted already. By the end of the week there was time to move from the hotel to her friend's house.

Before moving day she had her last romantic evening with Pierre. Since she was still using the hotel room. Then it would be less practical to be together. Saturday afternoon was passing quickly she was very busy at the shop. There was an unusual shopping day. It had seemed every customer came to shop.

Emily ended up being very exhausted.

All of the days to go out in the romantic evening but she had to forget about she was feeling in that moment. Finally the time came for her to leave.

"Bonsoir Madame."

"Bonsoir Emily." Emily then closed the door after her putting the closed sign at the door.

Quickly she walked towards the hotel. She opened the door she began to get ready for an evening. She takes a five minutes shower and washed her hair. Then got out from the bathroom. Already she was a bit, behind. But she hoped that Pierre would be late. She looked at the closet but there wasn't much to choose. But she had a very sensuous dress she slipped it in. She was ready for an evening out. She dabbed a little perfume on herself. She came down to the lobby and looked to see if Pierre was there. But he wasn't. She waited for him to arrive. When he came he brought a lovely rose for her. Pierre kissed Emily gently on her lips. It had been a whole week without seeing each other. They were anxious for the evening he apologizes for being late.

"Perdon moi Emily." They both walk to the car he opened the door. "Merci." Then he drove away. He told her the evening would be a very special one.

Pierre drove towards the Right Bank by the end of the Pont de l'Alma for the evening cruise and dinner. He parked the brown Porsche. Pierre and Emily held hands walking down to the quay towards the Bateaux Mouches for the evening dinner in the Seine River. They made a perfect couple the evening was theirs a romantic place and different…

"Bonsoir Mademoiselle." The garcon said good evening and showed their table.

Pierre chose something very wonderful which they ate and French red wine. The night was wonderful they passed through the famous places. She had been before but in the daytime.

"Emily comment ca va vous?"

"Bien Pierre mais je suis peu fatigue."

They toasted the long glasses touched. What a wonderful evening, it has been and view and also fantastic French pastries. Emily wasn't worried about her figure. On the end of their dinner Pierre chose an espresso while Emily had a café au lait.

The boat returned to the starting point. The stepped out from the boat. They walked up to the street level. They stopped, emotional and very physical. Pierre held Emily's hand and took her close to her. They kissed deeply and Emily felt butterflies in her stomach.

Fifteen

It had been along time since she had felt that great feeling. Both were very in much in love. She felt his arms holding her tightly. Those were going to be one of those days. Dinner had been very romantic; a night cruising in the Seine. The sky was visible to the naked eye and she saw the tiny stars in the distance. Emily hadn't the chance to see them often.

"Pierre il estest. une nuit amoureuse."

"Oui ma Cherie Emily."

They both stayed where they were leaning against the wall. They kissed, as they wanted to stay together. Then it was time to leave. They walked back to the car. Pierre drove back to the hotel. Silently they took the elevator.

Pierre opened the door and at last they were alone. Emily turned in the table lamp it, there was light in the room. Pierre walked towards Emily.

"Oui Emily viens ici ma amour." Emily walked closely to Pierre she put her arms around him. She felt his wonderful body his feelings towards her. He kissed her tenderly in her lips. They made love to each other all night. Then for a while they weren't be seeing each other for a period of time.

The both were exhausted they a very physical night. She lay silently there and slowly got up from bed. She was wearing her silky camisole with the matching panty. She wrapped it around her matching robe.

She looked outside it was going to be nice sunny winter Sunday. Pierre was still asleep meanwhile Emily was looking out through the window the streets were empty. Then she went to pick her underwear then chose something comfortable to wear. She slipped into her blue jeans and warm sweater.

The day would be a very busy one it was the moving day. She got dressed and ready for breakfast. Then she walked towards the bed she leaned over and kissed him in his cheek. He still didn't move and kept in sleeping. Then went to the bathroom for a warm bath. Afterwards she wrapped herself in a white towel and a small white towel in her head. Then she dried her hair with the hair dryer while she was drying her hair a lot of thoughts were in her mind.

She wondered how she was going to get along in her new place. She had a full schedule it didn't matter much. She slipped into her blue jeans and a sweater moments later. She came out from the bathroom. Although all that time still Pierre was asleep. He has been working hard and was working in one of the biggest hotels in Paris.

Emily was getting hungry so she decided it was time to have breakfast. Then she ordered breakfast for two meanwhile, she hoped Pierre would awaken by himself. She put the receiver down.

Pierre opened his eyes. He stretched his arms. Then he looked to his right side and saw Emily standing theretheir…"Bonjour Emily. Viens ici mon amour."

"Bonjour Pierre."

Emily came closer to Pierre he pulled her towards her. He kissed her deeply with so much passionate. Then lay there motionless for a long time until there was a knock at the door. Emily remember that was their breakfasts…

"C'est notre petite-dejeuner Pierre."

"Oui."

"Bien Emily. Allez ouvrir la porte."

While Emily, walked to the door. Pierre quickly got up and went towards the bathroom. She opened the door the garcon came in with the tray into his hands. Emily told him to leave at the table and she sign the bill and tipped him.

"Merci Mademoiselle." Afterwards she closed the door.

Meanwhile Pierre was getting ready and after fifteen minutes he came out. Already Emily was setting down and waiting for him. Then moments later they began their breakfasts. Everything smelled fresh and tasted good. After a nice dinner a good breakfast would be a nice idea. That was Emily thoughts.

"Bon…bon Emily."

"Oui Pierre."

Emily smiled at Pierre they were enjoying their breakfasts. The warm and buttered croissants tasted good and Emily had three croissants. Pierre ate one while he preferred coffee. Meanwhile under the table there was movement. Emily was touching Pierre's leg, rubbing her foot against his hairy leg. She was enjoying touching him.

"Oui ma Cherie."

They finished eating and Pierre walked beside Emily. He took her hand and slowly she got up. Then closely they embraced so tightly they kissed deeply. Moments, later Pierre carried Emily in his arms. He lay her in the bed. Gently he lay on top of her. They began to make passionate love. Slowly he undressed her. There was a wonderful feeling between the two of them. Each time they got involved there was something special. He really cared for her and they both were deeply involved physically.

Two hours later both walked out from the hotel. Emily had everything packed, as she left the clothes needed for the morning and her books. Pierre took her to where she was going to stay. Both looked at the room and it was all right for her and has enough space for herself.

"Bien Emily." He approved the room, which seemed to be fine.

Emily told Madame she was moving in in the next day. She was leaving her personal belongings there.

"Oui Mademoiselle."

Emily asked about Helene she was out with her boyfriend. She was happy because Emily was moving in. She thanked Madame. Then left with Pierre.

Pierre had a surprise for Emily. Pierre drove away from the city towards the countryside. It was a lovely day to get away from the city.

They drove for thirty minutes until he stopped at one of those country restaurants. There were a few cars parked around the place were surrounded by trees.

It was still a nice fall day but in the cool side. The surroundings were so peaceful a country restaurant frequented from a lot of Parisians. Their busiest season was the summer but towards the fall and winter months there was no need for reservations.

Emily got out from the car she stretched her legs for a while she walked around the parking lot.

Meanwhile Pierre walked inside of the restaurant to see if there was a table for two. He asked for a special table and took the liberty of ordering something very French and country.

Pierre walked out.

Emily was strolling around she was breathing the fresh air from all the beautiful surroundings.

He walked by her side and then put his arms around her waist.

They felt close to each other they stayed outside for a little bit. He had chosen already and it didn't matter at all. Emily told Pierre she loved the country. It made her relax and some times once.

It was good to get out from the city. Emily talked about her classes and her work. She was really enjoyable but at the same time it was hard on her.

Meanwhile Pierre had thoughts about setting a date for their marriage. But he knew that her school was important for her. They could wait and maybe they would work something out and in the other hand time seemed to pass quickly.

Then it was time to go in.

"Nous allons entre Emily."

"Oui Pierre."

They walked inside of the restaurant and it was very such country. The maitre d' showed their table. They sat down.

Pierre chose an Beaujolais wine, which tasted fruity.

Moments later the waiter brought the wine and showed to Pierre. He tasted and then said yes. Then the waiter poured into Emily's glass afterwards to Pierre. While they waited for the main course Pierre entertained Emily with his stories back when he was back in his school days.

They both laugh at each other they promised to each other to meet more often even if it was just for short while however it was possible.

Then the garcon came with their lapin de garenne aux herbes. Right away Emily looked at the plate and this must tasted good.

She tasted…"Oui Pierre. C'est bon."

They ate slowly they toasted their gourmet food. They slowly sipped their wine until there was none.

They had some good desserts they chose mousse au chocolate. Lunch had been superb afterwards Pierre had an espresso and Emily café au lait.

By the time they completed their wonderful lunch it was already the middle of the afternoon. But it was all right because it was Sunday.

After they got in the car Pierre drove around for a little while but he didn't say a word. Pierre drove around for a little while but he didn't say a word. Pierre also had a surprise for her. He came near a side road which road, which led to a hidden house. Pierre drove inside he passed to these huge trees and a lot of area. There were only green bushes.

It was a very typical French house in the countryside. At one side of the house there were two small cars parked. At the moment Emily looked at Pierre also had a wondering where he would take her.

The surroundings were very quiet. Then a dog stopped. He recognized and came running. Pierre still hadn't told her anything both walked up to the main door. He knocked at the door and waited a few minutes before someone answer.

A woman opened the door and she was surprised by the visit…"Entre Pierre…Emily."

Emily's recognized Pierre's mother. Pierre smiled at Emily both walked into the reading room.

Pierre's father was reading the French newspaper Le Monde. Pierre's father was surprise too. However Pierre wants to visit he usually calls. Pierre wanted to surprise his parents.

Pierre embraced his parents and Emily embraced his parents and Emily embraced also Madame and shake Monsieur. They all were glad to see each other. It was a really a big surprise.

Madame Nickesse went into the kitchen and later came out with a tray with a plate full of French pastries and a pot of coffee.

They talked for a little while then Pierre's mother went to show the house. Meanwhile Pierre spoke to his father.

Emily liked what she saw it. .

A half an hour later their parents came into the reading room. Emily showed them her ring. Everyone was very happy. Afterwards they said their goodbye. Then they left. When they arrived in Paris it was dark.

Pierre suggested for them to have some light food before going back to the hotel…"Oui Pierre.

C'est bien avec moi." They agreed, then Pierre stopped by a small restaurant. They chose a small place in the Avenue des Champs-Elysees. The place was opened in Sundays.

Two hours later they were in the lobby of the hotel. Emily picked the key and asked for the bill. She would be checking out in the morning. It would take a couple minutes both sat down while waiting.

The receptionist called Emily. There wasn't much Pierre then took his wallet and pay the bill.

Then they took the elevator up to the room.

Emily was happy and at that moment they walked in. They began making passionate caresses. Pierre throw himself all over Emily. They kissed slowly began to make love. There was a heat wave between the two of them. But it was then time to Pierre to leave He had to work in the next day and Emily would have to go to her classes. Emily wrote down her new address and telephone number of the house where she was staying. They would be in touch.

Pierre kissed her tenderly on her lips. Slowly he walked towards the door…"Au revoir Emily."

"Au revoir Pierre."

Then Pierre left.

It was a bit earlier to retire for the evening. She went back to do her portfolio. It wasn't so easy to do it. She had to force herself in working and to come with fresh ideas. She was sketching with her soft pencil on the white paper. She was drawing a two piece outfit. The skirt was short at the knee and a long jacket with straight lines. She defined with more details in her sketch. There was a back slit in the skirt and a zipper with a button. The jacket was three quarters with side pockets. But her mind was somewhere else she looked at her hand. She was admiring the ring. The pearl had an unusual shape. Then she went back to her sketches for a bit longer. At least she wanted to complete an outfit and a lot of questions went inside. She was doing the sketches she had to know those answers.

After a while it was done. She put it away in her black portfolio and tied the two black strings attached. She was doing the sketches she had to know those answers.

She had her nightgown in she took her matching robe. Then turned the lights off and she fell asleep. The night seemed to pass quickly it turned into dawn. Emily got up and took a shower and then got dressed. But she had time to have breakfast in a way to her classes.

Before she left the room she checked if she was leaving something behind. Then she closed the door and came to the lobby and hand in the key.

"Au revoir."

"Merci Monsieur. Au revoir."

Emily stepped into the street and towards the metro. By the time she got to school. The first person she saw was Helene…"Bonjour Helene."

"Bonjour Emily."

Both walked in to theirthere first class. The day had progress until was time to leave for her work. She waved to Helene. She said au revoir until the late afternoon.

Madame was happy to see her. It seemed to be a quiet day and the whole time, she was there not too many customers came in. She helped Madame to open new boxes from new clothing that had came in.

She helped Madame to open new boxes clothing that had come in.

Madame looks at her hand she saw the ring. She asked about if it was her engagement ring.

"Oui Madame."

After a long day she left. It took her half an hour for her to arrive at Helene's place.

Emily hadn't eaten anything and by the time she was tired. She rang the doorbell. Helene came to answer.

"Bonsoir ma cherie amie. Entre s'il vous plait."

"Merci Helene."

"Comment va vous Emily."

"Ah! Je suis fatigue Helene."

The two classes mates walked to the kitchen where Madame de Madeleine was cooking dinner.

"Bonsoir Mademoiselle."

Madame Madeleine asked if she wanted to have dinner with them. She said yes. She knew that that the food must be good. Emily notice in Helene had another younger sister and a brother. After the dinner Emily said good night and went up to her room. There she had clean towels and the bed sheets with two extra blankets. Emily changed and then began to de herself o her homework.

Moments later she turned in.

The days passed quite fast than she expected. Her work became much more. She seemed to be occupied with her work and plus her extra assignments. She tried very hard and most of the time she talked to Pierre by telephone.

Once a while she would give herself a real break by going out with him. But most the time she didn't spend anything engaged in her sexual pleasures. She enjoyed before but her work didn't permitted and plus the part time job. She kept her time very busy. Madame really liked her and she saw that the customers really liked her. Time has been passed very well. By the middle of the year they began to work in their designs for the fashion show towards the end of the semester.

Everything was coming well from what she expected. So was her personal portfolio. She was pleased with what she had accomplished in her portfolio.

Although it wasn't complete and she wanted to keep a secret even from her new friend Helene.

Sometimes the two girls went out together for coffee. Emily had the urge to tell her friend. It was hard for Emily to be able to separate the time from school then was her part time job and Pierre.

But some times she had to give herself a break so she could function better in both in her life plus in school. Her friend Helene was lucky she didn't needed to work so she had more time than Emily.

Emily sometimes saw Helene with her boyfriend going out she wanted also to go out more often with Pierre. But she couldn't do it her time was very much limited.

Then upon came an occasion a long weekend, which Emily didn't have to work, and her class worked was very little.

She made plans to spend with Pierre but she wanted to know if he was also free.

The days began to get warmer it was the spring season. A beautiful time to be in love in Paris.

It was late in the evening of Friday that she wasn't working. She went looking for Helene mother for the permission to make a local telephone call. Then she made the call. But Pierre wasn't at his apartment she tried at his work he wasn't there either.

Then she left the message at his work with his friend.

She told him who she was and the other French man say he would pass the message in.

Emily's waited for Pierre to call. Since she had arrived early from the boutique. She waited for a while she was by herself in her room. When Helene came knocking at the door…"Oui entre."

Helene came in in she wondered if her friend wanted to go out with her. Emily told her she was waiting for Pierre call. Maybe if he call in a while she would be waiting for another half an hour. Then, if there is no call. She would go out with Helene.

"Bien Helene."

Helene left. Emily went back to her sketches her hard work would be paid off later on. Her portfolio was coming well.

Suddenly there was another knock at the door…"Oui."

"C' estest. Madame."

"Entre." Madame told her she had a telephone call from someone named Pierre…"Merci Madame."

Emily came down right away to answer it…

…"Hello Pierre."

"Hello Emily. Comment ca va vous?"

"Je suis bien mon amour."

They began speaking then Emily asked if he was working the weekend. But the answer was in half.

Pierre told Emily that he had to work in Saturday all day and Sunday morning. But the rest of the Sunday and Monday he was free. Emily told him she didn't have to work that weekend. They made plans to spend the rest of the Sunday afternoon and Monday. Emily suggested going out some place in the country. Pierre agreed with her so he would spend the rest weekend together.

"Au revoir Pierre."

"Au revoir Emily."

She put the receiver down. Then she looks for Helene wondering if she had left already. Emily walked to the kitchen and asked her mother if she was still around the house.

Helene mother told her that she was in her room. But she was going out with her boyfriend. Emily waited she saw her and asked if the offer was still good. She was free to go.

"Oui Emily. Viens ici."

Emily quickly went up to get her handbag and her sweater. She came down and both girls left. Helene told Emily she was meeting Jean at the café.

But she told her where they were meeting. Helene took Emily to the Deux-Magots. She was surprised. Emily heard about the café since she has been in Paris. She hadn't yet come in. Helene was looking for Jean.

But she had seen him. Then both sat down in one of the empty tables.

"Oui Mademoiselle." The garcon asked what they wanted.

"Je prend une tasse de café au lait s'il vous plait." Emily chose her usual but for Helene she asked for something else.

"Espresso s'il vous plait."

"Merci Mademoiselle."

Helene was looking always in every direction to see if she could see Jean. He was late which was no surprise to Helene. Any time they met in some place he would always be late. Then five minutes later the garcon brought the two coffees…"Merci."

At that moment Jean showed up…"Bonsoir Helene."

Jean kissed her on he rosy lips. He didn't see that Emily was there. He kissed Helene.

"Oui ma Cherie."

"Perdon nous Emily. Je vous presente Jean. Ici c'est ma amie Emily." Helene introduces Emily to Jean.

"Enchante Emily."

Jean sat down and he called the waiter. The garcon that was serving their table approached.

"Oui Monsieur."

"Un espresso et un cognac."

"Bien Monsieur."

They began speaking to each other in English. Emily told how got to Paris and the rest up to date. Minutes later the garcon brought the espressos and the cognac…"Merci."

After a while Jean told the two of them if they wanted to go anywhere. They didn't mind staying where they were for a bit longer. They didn't mind staying where they were for a bit longer. Emily and Helene order a cup of delicious ice cream while Jean another French cognac.

After a while Jean paid everything he spoke about his work for a while too. They were laughing with each other. They were having so much fun until was time to leave. They took the metro to Helene house. Upon arrival Emily left the two alone and went in.

"Bon nuit."

"Bien bon nuit Emily…"

Moments, later Emily was in bed she turned the lights off. Meanwhile Helene and Jean were together. They were kissing enchanted in each other arms. They stayed a long while in the street.

A new day arrived for Emily some how she was awake at the same time usual. But soon she looked at the time. She went back to sleep for a little longer.

She really slept for another two hours.

Suddenly she was awakened for the second time. She was feeling hungry. Quickly she got up and went to the bathroom.

She took a quick shower and got dressed. She was ready to go out. But she was already at the bottom of the stairs when she had remembered she had forgot her sketchbook and notepad. By then Helene was coming out from her bedroom…

"Bonjour Helene ca va bien."

"Oui et vous?"

Emily told Helene she was going out for a big breakfast. She wondered if she wanted to come too. She had the whole day free. Helene accepted the offer. She got up herself too. She had to get her handbag.

Moments later the two friends left.

Emily liked the Deux-Magots she told Helene. She preferred to go back to the same place she told Helene. Helene said it was fine with her it didn't matter where they went.

Upon their arrival they sat down it was a sunny morning. A good one to be outside. Emily chose two croissants with and a large cup of café au lait.

Meanwhile Helene wasn't hungry so she had only one café au lait. She was meeting Jean for lunch. Emily took out her sketchbook she began to sketch and write a few notes down. Her ideas for outfits and fabrics she watched the crowds going by.

She was trying something very exciting. She was working for the fashion show for the school that was approaching soon. She had drafted the patterns. She was presenting three different pieces of clothing. But she would have to do her sewing after her classes.

Since she didn't had a sewing machine. But at the same time Emily wondered if the school would let her borrow the sewing machine. She was working Emily's time was very limited.

"Excuse-moi Mademoiselle." The waiter brought the fresh croissants and the coffee…"Merci."

Emily had her croissants while Helene has her coffee. Helene saw Emily eating and changed her idea of having nothing. She call out the garcon asked him for a croissant.

"Oui Mademoiselle."

They talked about their classes. Helene has been staying after hours, since she was behind with her patterns. They enjoyed each others company but Helene had to leave she paid her share. Emily was alone. She done some sketches meantime she orders another café au lait…"Merci."

Emily had accomplished a lot. She needed a few ideas that she got. Later in she would do them in a larger scale. Afterwards Emily left. She walked down to the metro. She needed a few essentials so she went shopping at Boulevard Haussman.

She browsed the different departments and she bought what she needed. Then walked in the boulevard she was passing by a new stand she brought a magazine. Then went inside of a restaurant. She chose an omelet with ham and a green salad. She asked for a chilly Perrier.

Emily relaxed because she knew the following week would be a really busy one.

After her lunch she went to one of the side café in the Avenue Champs-Elysees. She sat down which it was a calm spring day. Lovers were every whereeverywhere kissing and holding hands. At the same time Emily was missing Pierre he was in her mind. But he wasn't too far away but at that moment he seemed to be a long distance away from her. But he wasn't at all. She had her coffee then left. It had been half of a day different than the normal ones.

Emily took the metro back to Helene house. Their surroundings were in the old part of the city. On a narrow street, with those huge windows with antique, rails with huge pots of plants, and flowers. The house had a high ceiling but some of the rooms were small others were really large.

She went up to her room and decided to rest for a little ceiling but some of the rooms were small others were really large.

She went up to her room and decided to rest for a little while before resuming her sketches.

She lay in top of the bed and she fell asleep.

Sixteen

Somehow she slept more than she wanted too. When she opened her eyes saw that it was dark outside. When she noticed the time she was feeling hungry. She felt like going some where she went to freshen up a bit. Then came downstairs to look for Madame. She wondered if they had their dinner.

She called out loud. Suddenly she heard a voice…"Un minute." Then Madame showed up everyone had left. She asked Madame if she could make something to eat. She said yes because she didn't eat well. She would cook something for them two.

They talked for a while Madame was preparing something. Then they ate and then she thanked Madame. Then she went anywhere. Emily went back to her sketches she was close to finishing her portfolio. But she was worried about how she was getting a sewing machine. She was worried about how she was getting a sewing machine. She needed it to be able to complete her outfits for the show.

Soon she would go to back to work she would asked Madame if she had a sewing machine.

Maybe she knew someone would have one and let her borrow. She had two more sketches to finish. Then she picked up her book to study her notes. She was having soon the testes. But in four weeks there will be a fashion show. Soon she could get her hands in the sewing machine. She would ask Madame for two or three days off. She would hope she wouldn't mind at all. She would work in the summer months but the boutique would be closed in August for holidays.

It was already one o'clock in the morning. She put her work away. The next day she would be meeting Pierre.

Emily chose a few outfits and accessories and a few essentials for the rest of the weekend. Then it was time to go back to sleep. Quickly she fell asleep. All night she dreamed about the time she would be spending with Pierre.

A new day just arrived the sunshine through the window. She was awake in around the middle of the morning. She took a quick shower and got dressed. Pierre was meeting her for lunch. She walked out into the street. She saw Helene coming in.

"Bonjour Helene. Comment ca va vous?"

"Bien merci."

Then Emily left in the worry she walked for ten minutes where was a small café. When she got there the place was full. She had to wait for a moment until someone got up.

Emily was giving up and was about to walk away.

When someone got up and she had right away went to the table. As soon as she sat down the garcon approached her...

"Oui Mademoiselle."

"Oui je prend une tasse de café au lait et un petit pain."

A period of five minutes later the garcon brought her breakfast..."Merci."

She had her second cup of coffee she sketchpad. She was feeling marvelous.

She smiled at everyone who happened to pass by. She was feeling wonderful from being in Paris again.

She had remembered the first time she had met him. There was the attraction of his baby blue eyes and his rosy cheeks. He spoke gently in his native language.

She was waiting for the time to pass it always passed quickly. She was waiting for the time to pass it always passed quickly. She paid for her breakfast. Then went back to the house. When she arrived at the house moments later she heard a car horn sounded twice. She looked and saw Pierre. She came down and went across the street. Pierre rolled down the window of his car.

"Bonjour Emily. Comment ca va vous ma cherie."

"Bien Pierre." They greed each other. Then Emily spoke to Pierre she was going inside for a moment to get her weekend bag…"Oui Emily."

Quickly Emily across the street again. Then went inside of the house she walked up to her room. She changed her clothing and step inside of the bathroom. She brushed her hair and looked in the mirror she put lipstick in. Then came out from house and smiled she opened the door of the car and step in.

Emily kissed Pierre their emotions were deep they kissed and embraced each other. After a long week without seeing each other. There was a moment of silence then Pierre drove away to their destination.

Pierre had something special in his mind. He had some reservations for two. After an hour of driving they arrived in a town. They stopped at a spa resort. They went inside. Afterwards they went to their room…"Oh! OuiPierre. C'etait fantastique."

"Oui ma Cherie."

They embraced with passion and they made love right away. There was no city sounds only country ones, which were so peaceful. Pierre kissed her she felt the pressure of his body in hers.

She knew he loved each and every moment they spent together. After satisfying each other they took a shower but Emily took her time. Then, after getting ready again both, went out to the street for a bit of fresh air. They held their hands they were very much, a couple inlovein love. They walked in the active area of the town they saw a restaurant. They stopped outside to read the menu the food seemed appealing to them and also there was a large crowd inside.

They stepped in…"Bonjour Mademoiselle…Monsieur."

The maitre d' showed a table for two he left two menus to look out. They browsed through the menu but they chose something, local which, it was something special of that restaurant. Pierre chose a red wine the waiter brought a bottle and opened. He approved…"Oui."

After a while the waiter brought a soupe a la Juliene. Afterwards the navarin, which is a dish, made of mutton stew with potato and onions.

The food tasted delicious then Pierre asked for a second bottle of Bordeaux. They toasted again for the two wonderful days.

"Pour nous."

"Oui pour nous."

After a long lavish lunch they topped it with two coffees. They walked with each other around the area.

Time passed and both went back to the spa. Then they went for a deep message, and later in they would be joining at the whirlpool. Emily hadn't felt relaxed for so long even Pierre was distressed from his work.

They had met at the whirlpool and stayed for a while until both had enough. Then they went to different changing rooms. Afterwards they met again at the lounge.

"Bien Pierre. Maintenant nous allons mange quelque chose."
"Oui, nous pouvons allez, au le restaurant. Que ce que vous pense Emily."
"Bien Pierre."

They went up to their room to change something suitable for dinner. Later they came down they walked to the restaurant. It was a small town but with a lot of restaurants because of the famous spa.

There were a lot of people coming from everywhere.

Although. The restaurant was full but soon they were sitting down at the table.

The maitre d' showed the menu he pointed out some sugges-tions…"Merci." She sat down meanwhile she looked at the menu and Pierre glanced through the wine list.

"Oui Monsieur."

Emily told Pierre about her work and the fashion show. She was looking for a sewing machine for her to finish her outfits for the show. Pierre spoke also about his work.

They chose something wonderful. After dinner Emily had a Port and Pierre an old age French brandy. Emily told Pierre she had one more year. Then she will try to find work a designer. Emily spoke about how important was the fashion show because there will be a lot of the photographers and designers looking for a new and young assistants.

She was optimistic because of her portfolio, which was coming well. She smiled at Pierre and he was happy for her. They finished their glasses and were time to leave. They walked back they looked to the stars which could be seen clearly.

Pierre got the key and it seemed that everyone came at once for theirs keys.

"Bien Emily nous allons."

"Oui Pierre."

A short walk to the elevator and moments later they were at their room. The furniture was dated back to King Louis XIV. Emily took a moment to undress she slipped was into her lacy nightgown and at the same time she was feeling sensuous.

When she returned to the room there he was handsome. Pierre got up he came to her then took her in his arms. He lifted her in the air then gently lay her in bed. Slowly they began making love to each other. They were in touch physically.

But she was always careful; she took precautions. After all night full of excitement they fell asleep. It was much quieter there. The morning arrived with the sound of the birds then Emily opened her eyes and got up. Pierre took a shower then went down for some aerobics and swim. She felt a note for Pierre. She closed the door silently then came down.

She was having a message when a receptionist handed her a note. There was a moment, which the message therapist, stop so she could read the note. Pierre wrote…after the swimming pool they will meet for breakfast…

An hour later they were having breakfast they made plans for the day. Pierre told her before going straight to Paris they will stop at his parents.

"Oui je prend autre tasse de café s'il vous plait."

"Bien Mademoiselle."

They sat there for a while then left the table.

"Quand est-ce que nous partons pour Paris?"

Emily wanted to know when they would be leaving.

"Emily pendant une heure." He said around one hour.

They went up to the room to pack the few belongings. Later they went up to leave. Pierre made a call to his mother. They would be passing by there later in belongings. Later they were ready to leave. Pierre made a call to his mother. They would be passing by there later in the afternoon.

Madame suggested they would stay for dinner.

Madame said also they will make an early dinner…

…"Bien Pierre mon, fils."

Pierre said yes. Afterwards he made another call to the room services. He asked for a bottle of champagne. Minutes later there was a knock at the door…"Merci."

Pierre thanked the garcon and signed the bill. Emily was surprise by the champagne because she didn't hear him, call. Pierre unscrewed the cork they toasted to each other…"Salut."

They slowly sipped the bubbly and they laugh with each other. They both were happy.

Emily in her next few weeks she would be extreme busy. But soon her classes would be finishing then there more time.

After a second glass of champagne they were up to make love one more time. As their passionate ran wild Pierre kissed Emily.

Two hours later they were in the way to the house of Pierre's parents. But they stop in one of the country cafes. They sat down and a man with a white jacket came over. Meanwhile Emily excused herself she went to the ladies room. When she came back there were a café au lait and a croissant.

There were always seemed to stop in a way to Paris or somewhere else. "Merci Pierre."

She thanked him for him ordering one croissant although she had a big breakfast. She was feeling a little hungry.

Later in they would be arriving at the country house. Finally, they arrived, the tall greens and there were a lot of green bushes. Emily stepped out of the car…"Oui bien. Nous sommes ici Emily."

"Oui Pierre."

They walked up to the front entrance and knocked at the door, which had one of the old doorbells.

Moments the huge wood door opened it was his mother…"Bonsoir Pierre…Ah…ma Cherie Emily." His mother than embraced Pierre and then Emily…

"Entre." His father was sitting down in the back of the house in the garden. Emily and Pierre walked out in the back.

Meanwhile Pierre's mother was finishing the last touches in the dinner. Emily stayed outside with Monsieur while Pierre came inside of the house to speak to his mother.

He asked her about her sewing machine if she still had it. Emily was working in various projects she needed for the fashion show.

Madame was glad to lend to Emily. Then Pierre went out to the garden. Then it was time for dinner everyone sat down at the table. Pierre's father poured down the red Bordeaux and he carved the roast lamb. They had a wonderful dinner and to top of all a tasty dessert. Then it was time to leave for Paris.

Madame went to one of the room's in the back of the house to get her sewing machine.

Emily was surprise when she saw her carrying a sewing machine…"Ah! Madame, Merci."

"Bien Emily."

Emily was grateful she was able to finish her outfits. Madame told her she didn't needed it any longer.

She could use long she wanted. They said their good-bye.

"Au revoir Pierre…Emily." His mother embraced them both.

"Au revoir." They both said and waved. Pierre drove away. It didn't take long for Pierre to arrive in Paris.

"Bien ma Cherie. Nous sommes ici."

"Oui Emily. Peutre nous allons au café."

"Oui Pierre."

Then Pierre instead of leaving by the house. They drove away. He parked the car. They held their hands and walked to the tiny café and it was very cozy. They sat down. Then the waiter came to the table.

"Oui Mademoiselle…Monsieur."

"Un café au lait et un espresso."

"Merci."

Afterwards they left Pierre drove her back. When they arrive they took the sewing machine and the weekend bag. Pierre helped carry the tings up to her room.

Then both came, out again they stayed closed to the car. They kissed and embraced each other.

"Je vous t'aime ma Emily."

"Oui moi aussi Pierre. Je vous aime beaucoup."

Once more they kissed and said au revoir to each other. Emily went up to her room she got ready to bed.

Moments later she had fallen asleep

A new day began for Emily. Quickly it was time to get ready for school. The fashion show was getting closer. She came every day from her work back to the house. She didn't have time those days to go any-where. She didn't have time those days to go anywhere. She had brought always some kind of ready cooked food. She was spending all her evenings in sewing. At the same time she had completed her portfolio. But no one had seen it and she was pleased with it.

Finally the day had arrived. Emily was nervous and so her friends. The show would be in the gymnasium. The crowds were approaching and setting in their places.

Emily was in the back of the stage. She wondered if Pierre was among the crowd. She had told him when it would begin. But, there was less of an hour away for the show to begin. At the back of the gymnasium were the journalists and the photographers.

She wasn't sure if it was all right or not.

She had nothing to lose maybe it will be good for her.

"Mademoiselle…Vous pouvais parle avec moi."

"Oui Monsieur."

The interview didn't took longer the reporter walked away and at the same time Pierre came over to Emily."

"Tres bien Emily." "Merci Pierre."

They embraced and he kissed her slightly on her lips. Then they walked around and made conversation with the Emily's friends. She presented Pierre to her classmates and teachers.

After they stayed a while and the reception was coming to an end. Everyone was leaving. Then it was time for Pierre and Emily to depart too. The school days were closing for another teachers.

Helene stayed a bit longer with Jean. Emily said au revoir.

Pierre took Emily to Le Fouquet's for an evening out just the two of them. She not had a good meal for so long however the dinner with Pierre made forget all that work she had done.

The evening had turned out to be a very successful for everyone. In the few days they would know how the fashion critics responded to the fashion show.

Pierre left the car a little bit further from the restaurant because was one of the busiest evenings.

They had to wait for a table meanwhile they waited at the bar. They both had a red Martini's.

Emily spoke about all the nights of her hard work. She stopped going to the restaurants and having sandwiches. But it paid off she was happy.

"Oui ma Cherie."

"Et vous Pierre comment va vous?"

Emily wondered how he was feeling these days soon everything will change. Moments the maitre d' came to tell the table was ready…"Monsieur etait prete."

"Merci."

The maitre d' showed them to their table…."Merci."

The rest of the night went smoothly. Pierre then drove Emily to his apartment. They stayed the whole night.

The lasts days of classes went well. It ended in the middle of the month June meanwhile the last day of her classes she went to register for the next term in September.

The group organized a party by the lunch hour a few went shopping at supermarket. Then later in everyone was set for the party. Emily didn't needed to go to work.

Madame had given her day off.

The next day she began working longer hours. Also she had longer breaks too. Emily spoke about the fashion show then she got good reviews and showed to Madame.

"Bien Emily."

"Merci Madame."

Madame was impressed with Emily. Madame's customers also liked the way Emily spoke to them and how they helped them. After a few days working full time Emily decided to show her portfolio to Madame. Madame congratulated her work well done.

Madame afterwards spoke about a friend she had who knew a fashion designer. She would show Emily's portfolio to him.

Madame asked her if she didn't mind her leaving her portfolio…"Oui Madame."

Madame would be in contact with her friend. Meanwhile Emily went back to the customers. Suddenly there were a lot of the regular customers in the boutique.

"Merci Madame." Emily thanked one of her customers…"Au revoir Mademoiselle."

Then it seemed a day for the customers to come in. But there was time for Emily's lunch break. Then she went for her lunch she walked by a close bistro. She calmed down for a bit she relaxed for a while. She had a green salad then for the main course grilled chicken.

Afterwards she went back to the boutique. On the way she bought a local magazine at the news-stand.

When she looked at the widow of the boutique, which needed to be change to a new concept. She had to arrange into a new theme. She looked at the window and thoughts came into her head. Then she wrote down all the pieces of clothing and accessories for her to do the view display.

Emily was displaying the pieces of clothing in the window meanwhile a small crowd began to form outside. They were pleased to see what she was doing. She smiled to them. They have finished all her window she stepped outside. It seemed to be all right and then a few minutes she opened the shop. There weren't customers for a while she finished tidying up.

On the afternoon she had not to many customers meanwhile Madame was very amazed by what Emily had done to the window display.

"Tres bien Emily."

Madame told her the good news she had for her. Her friend was going to be showing the portfolio to the designer by the end of the follow week. Then she will know.

She hadn't told Pierre about her portfolio she will tell him if she when would have good news. It will be a surprise for him.

After speaking to Madame she still had to do two more customers. Then it was time to close the boutique. Madame told Emily she could leave.

"Bonsoir Madame."

"Adieu Emily."

She went for dinner in the Latin Quarter she chose a place which had pasta. Her thoughts were always in the Pierre. Then the garcon asked if she wanted anything else.

"Mademoiselle c'est tous."

"Non…un café au lait. S'il vous plait."

"Bien Mademoiselle."

Emily was also thinking in her drawings and her ideas. How was she going to do it about her own life and sometimes their was a struggle in her mind.

"Merci." She thanked the garcon after he left the cup of coffee. After a lovely dinner it was time to go back to the house.

Seventeen

The days passed quickly Emily got anxious to know about her work. She was happy working with Madame and enjoyed her work.

Finally one day Madame arrived later than usual. She had good news for Emily. But she was busy with one client and soon there was no one else. Madame spoke to her...

"Emily j'avais bien."

Madame told her that her friend was a designer and she will show it. He was very curious about Emily's working had a lot of promising.

"Oui Madame. C'est vrai?" Emily wondered if it was true what she just heard.Afterwards he will be in touch with her by via the boutique. It was a privilege having some of her designs being at the same level as any famous designer.

Emily was so happy her face lit up with joy.

She thanked Madame for helping her. The designer had read the reviews from the fashion show. Emily told Madame she was working on the second portfolio.

"Merci Madame."

The morning was very busy Madame told her she could have an extra hour for lunch. She would be there to open the door..." Oui...Madame...merci."

When time came open for Emily to have lunch she tried to get in touch with Pierre. She wanted to have lunch with him. Of course he was free. He told her he would pick her up. She waited fifteen minutes then she heard a car horn.

There he was.

"Au revoir Madame."

"Au revoir Emily."

Emily step outside she smiled to Pierre afterwards she kissed him.

"Bonjour Pierre. Comment ca va vous?"

"Je suis bien merci et vous ma cherie?"

"Je suis tres heureuse." She said, to him she was really happy. He wonders right away, she must have good news.

Emily told Pierre she had an extra hour for lunch and had something especial to tell him. Pierre chose a romantic place for lunch. She hadn't been to that restaurant.

Pierre asked the wine waiter to bring a bottle of champagne. They had lobster for the main course.

She told him about her designs and Madame had helped her. Already she was working in her second portfolio. They finished their lunch Pierre began speaking. When was the appropriated date for their wedding he needed her and she needed him she told him the next time they meet. They will discuss that matter. They would see each other by the weekend.

After a long lunch Pierre took Emily back. Then they kissed and she got out from the car. They waved…"Au revoir."

Pierre speeded up his car and soon he had disappeared from her view she walked in and the boutique was full of clients. Madame was relief when she saw her to come in.

Emily began right away to help the customers.

Quickly the afternoon went fast, then it was time to close the boutique. Then she began to tidy up all the clothes. The racks were a mess there was a lot to do.

When she left the boutique was late around nine o'clock. Afterwards she stopped to eat a bagatelle sandwich with ham and cheese. Then she went back to the house. She opened the door Helene was coming out.

"Bonsoir Helene. Comment ca va vous?"

"Bien Emily."

"Je suis bien merci."

Helene asks her if she wanted to go out for coffee with her. Emily thanked her maybe next time. She had just arrived from her work and was very tired.

"Bien Emily je comprend…Au revoir."

Then she went inside of her room. It has been a long day. She was tired she realized she had been in contact with her parents. She began writing a letter to her mother, which took her three pages.

She sealed them.

A few minutes later she turned the lights off and went to sleep.

The summer months came and went; meanwhile Madame closed the boutique for the month of August for holidays. Although Pierre was working but in the weekends they tried to be together.

Emily had been working hours drawing and drawing and drafting. She chose the ones she liked and then she went shopping around Paris for the inexpensive fabrics.

She loved walking to be narrow streets and getting inside.

She had completed six outfits. She was proud of them too.

Emily had discussed her wedding plans she had promised she would talks about with him.

They made the decision in their wedding they chose the month of June in the follow year. She wanted a small simple wedding. She hoped that her parents would be there and her mother would come a month prior of her wedding. Pierre agreed that was a good idea.

A new month began and also the classes for the New Year. The year would be more intense and more work too. She was already ahead of her colleges. She began working with a designer for three hours every week. But she had less, hours to work at the boutique however she worked extra hours in Saturdays. She got in touched with her mother by writing. Her mother was happy for her and she for sure she would be there for her wedding and moral support.

Finally the day arrived for the beginning of her classes. The first day all met and they exchanged ideas and they talked about their holidays. Everyone was happy to see each other.

Emily by the beginning of the fall season some of the designs was entered in the fashion show.

She received a sum of money from her from her designs, which were sold in Madame boutique.

She was also getting a better salary from her work. She was selling a lot and Madame decided to reward her. Although she was closed to her classes however she could afford a bigger place to live in.

Since she couldn't do her work well at that place and sometimes she wanted to see Pierre she couldn't where she was. Emily had to work well she was used to. But she had to work well she was used to. But she had two fashion shows at the school one would be in winter and the other one would be at the end of the school year.

She began looking at the ads she wasn't being lucky. Emily saw less and less of Pierre.

Pierre wondered about Emily emotions if she had changed her mind.

The Christmas season was approaching meanwhile she had almost completed her outfits for the fashion show. But she couldn't do it with Madame's help because she asked if she could have less hours working there so she could finished her outfits. She would make it.

All off that time Pierre had seen her at all. He couldn't take it any longer so he decided to go see her at the house.

Pierre parked the car near the house. Then he approached the house and knocked at the hand knot. He waited for a few minutes then a woman came to answer.

"Oui Monsieur."

"Je peux parle avec Mademoiselle Emily."

"Un moment s'il vous plait Monsieur."

"Madame, c'est Pierre."

"Oui Monsieur."

Helene's mother walked up to the second floor she knocked at the Emily's door…"Oui…oui."

"Mademoiselle…Pierre etait la bas et il veux parle avec vous."

"Bien merci. Madame…J'allez…"

Madame came down and she told Pierre she would be coming down…."Merci Madame."

A lot of thoughts were running in Emily's head. She realized she had been so busy that she had neglected Pierre. She hadn't seen him for a long while. She was sewing her outfit and she put it away. Quickly brushed her hair and then came downstairs.

"Bonsoir Pierre comment ca va vous?"

He had answered with a negative response…"Bonsoir Emily. Je n'est-ce pas que dire a vous?"

Pierre didn't know it what to say to her at that point.

Emily knew it that it was absolutely wrong.

A few wet tears came down in her cheeks. There were no words between them two.

"Oh! Ma Emily. Je t'aime beaucoup. Je pardonne."

Pierre had forgiven her and he held closed to him. She was glad he came to see her.

They kissed they wanted to make love. She could get away for a short time.

"Oui Pierre."

Emily picked her handbag and then they left. They were quiet as he drove towards to his apartment. He opened the door they walked inside. Immediately Pierre held her tight he kissed passionate. His heart began beat faster and faster. Emily was feeling so wanted then she was seducing him. Then he lifted her up in the air he walked to the bedroom and gently put her on the bed.

They made passionate and physical love. They were satisfied and both promised no matter how much work they had that they will make a little time to see each other. Then they kissed and Pierre took Emily back to the house.

"Au revoir Pierre."

"Au revoir Emily."

Pierre left. Emily walked up to her room meanwhile she went back to her work. The fashioned show would be in a couple days.

After working for two hours she finished what she was doing. She went out for a bite to eat by a close café.

It was getting darker and chilly. She sat down and soon the garcon asked her what she wanted.

"Oui Mademoiselle."

"Une bagatelle avec le jambo et le fromage s'il vous plait."

Moments later the garcon brought her sandwich and a Perrier…"Merci."

Quickly she finished eating and then paid and left.

She went in for her first class of the day. Already Helene had arrived and both greed each other. Then the teacher came in and the class began. The teacher asked of all of them how they were doing with their final touches.

On the afternoon classes were dealt with the technical information in the drafting and the whole idea of a construction of various types of fabric. Then there advantages of working with some and than others. By the last class was cut short so they could work on their garments.

Emily immediately went to the house.

She began working with the last garment but there was much sewing to be done in the garment. After a while she took a break and then called Pierre. He had answer yes he was free for dinner. They chose a place to meet at Grand Café Capucines. Emily took the metro to the Opera.

She looked and she hadn't seen Pierre.

She asked for a white bottle of wine. Then moments later the waiter showed the bottle and she said yes. At that point Pierre walked in and went directly to the table. He agreed Emily and kissed her in both cheeks.

"Bonsoir ma Cherie."

Then the waiter approached the table and poured wine into Pierre's glass. Pierre chose mussels a la mariniere. It is cooked with white shallots and a bit of parsley. Emily chose the same. They began eating Emily like it. Then Pierre asked for another bottle of wine. They enjoyed their dinner and they talked and finally they had their coffees.

Afterwards Pierre took Emily back to the house. Then they said good night to each other. He pulled Emily he held her around his arms and kissed her.

"Au revoir Pierre."

"Au adieu Emily."

She decided to do a little bit of work in her last garment. She was feeling relief because she was completing her outfits. Then she looked at her watch and saw it was time to go to bed.

The next day she overslept. Then she decided not to attend any her classes. Then late in that morning she went out to eat something.

She was coming downstairs Madame called her saying she had a letter "Merci Madame."

She went to her favorite cafe she sat down and opened her letter from her mother.

"Dear Emily…We hope you are fine. We are well and we have good news for you. We are planning to spend Christmas with you in Paris.

We have made all arrangements…"

At that point the garcon came with the two croissants. "Merci."

She would finish later in reading her mother's letter. After she ate everything she finished the letter. There was a small newsstand across the café she went to buy a newspaper. Then she returned back to the same table. She browsed through the ads for the apartment. But she looking at the ads there was nothing she seemed to be interested. She was about to give up and put the newspaper away. She saw a place in a good area that was close by the metro. It said that had certain features such a spacious room and bathroom. The price wasn't so bad, and it was closer to the boutique but was further away from the school. She circled for that place and would looked into it.

Moments later she left.

A few days passed meanwhile she was busy at the boutique for the festival season. Then the fashion show came. It was very successful. Emily was happy and Pierre was really glad for her. Her designs were also a success. Then the day came for her to go to the airport to get her parents. They pleased to see her. Emily saw them to come right away. They passed through the customs officials.

"Emily may dear how are you?"

"Mamma I am fine thank you."

Emily embraced her father…"How are you dad?"

"I am fine Emily. I am glad to see you Emily."

After they had greed each other. Emily helped her parents to get to there to the hotel. They had planned

Everything and their hotel reservations were in advance. They took a taxi to downtown of Paris from the airport Charles de Gaulle.

The taxi driver was requested to stop in front of the Holiday Inn at 10 place de Republic. They got out. The porter took their baggage. Emily paid the taxi driver. Then they checked in.

Moments later they were all up to their room. The room from was all right. Emily couldn't stay to long she had to go back to work. Her parents were at same time tired from the trip.

"How are you these days Emily?" Her father asked her. It has been along while before they had any contact.

"I have been very busy with my work the subjects that I have been taken in they are much harder. Although my designs of the first portfolio has been a success. So you see dad I have been occupied."

"How do you have time for yourself?" Her father asked her wondering if she had free time for herself.

"Emily…how is Pierre?"

"He is fine mother."

Emily couldn't stay to long she had to go back to work. They were all right.

"Mother…I have better be going. I will get in touch."

On Emily's tiny notebook she wrote down the telephone and room number. She embraced her parents then she left…"Good -bye mother…father."

Emily took the metro to the closest stop to the boutique. It was opened longer she had also longer hours.

"Bonjour Emily."

"Bonjour Madame."

Emily right away walked to the back of the boutique. She put down her handbag and slip out her coat.

Then she came out to the front. There was a crowd immediately so she began helping.

The boutique was open until nine o'clock. Later in she took a break she had something to eat. The afternoon was busy and well. Then later it was time to tidy up everything and leave.

Emily for the following days where important for her to see her parents much she could. She was planning the Christmas season she organized everything will be together.

By Saturday Emily had to work meanwhile she made the reservations. When eight o'clock arrived they all met at the lobby of the hotel. Pierre would meet her and her parents.

Finally she saw him entering the hotel and she got up walked towards Pierre.

"Bonsoir Pierre."

"Bonsoir ma Cher Emily…Comment ca va vous?"

"Je suis bien merci." The two of them walked back to Emily's parents.

Emily's father got up and greed Pierre" It is a nice to meet you sir." Pierre then greed Emily's mother. "Good evening Madame."

"Well it is nice to see you again Pierre."

After an introduction and a bit of a conversation they left in Pierre's car. The older couple sat in the back. Meanwhile Emily's father was admiring the view. It was his first visit to Paris.

Later Pierre arrived close to the restaurant. He looked for a space for him to park the car however he got lucky there was another driver moving out.

Moments later they all were walking to the restaurant.

"Bonsoir Madame…Mademoiselle…Monsieur…votre mon s'il vous plait."

Then maitre d' showed them the table…"Merci."

Pierre asked for a bottle of French champagne to celebrate of being together. They toasted the arrival of Emily's parents and their engagement.

Emily was happy because her parents were in Paris and at the same time it was the festival season. After dinner Pierre took all of them in the tour of the city. Then it was time for Pierre to take them to the hotel.

"Good night Pierre. It was wonderful." "Thank you Monsieur."

"Bon nuit Madame."

Afterwards Emily said good night to her parents. Then she would be in touch with them next day. Then Pierre took Emily back to the house. They arrived by the house he parked the car across the street. Pierre embraced Emily he hugged her tightly and gently kissed her.

Emily had missed Pierre she hadn't had not seen him much, she wanted.

Then out of the blue Pierre asked Emily if she wanted to spend a night with him. Then she would have the rest of the Sunday to enjoy with her parents. Maybe they could go sightseeing. Then was Emily thought about one minute or two, then she answered yes. But she would go up and get some of her essentials. Quickly she went inside of the house and up to her room. She picked an outfit and a few cosmetic essentials. Then ten minutes later she was opening the car door…"Oui ma Cherie."

"Oui Pierre. Nous allons maintenat."

When they arrived at front of his apartment building. Pierre parked the car and Emily stepped out she walked to the entrance and a few steppes behind were Pierre.

Then he opened the door for her he handed her hand in her weekend bag. Emily went to change her evening gown into her sexy camisole and her wrapped around the robe.

Meanwhile Pierre went to the kitchen and prepared a tray of various fruits and small sandwiches. When she came out she sat in the sofa and Pierre brought the tray with all goodies. He set it on the table and Emily was always amazed at the little things he did.

They sat in the sofa while they ate. After a while both went into the bedroom they made passionate love. Pierre held Emily gently he was so happy for having her at his side. It has been while. They made love all night until they both were very exhausted.

They both fell asleep in each other's arms. The new day began but in the rainy side and in a cold one. They slept late. Emily got up. Meanwhile Pierre was asleep. Emily took a long shower she relaxed.

When she came back from the bathroom Pierre was awake. He got up and wrapped his silky robe and then went to the kitchen. But first he was looking for Emily she wasn't anywhere in the apartment. But there was a note in the kitchen then she said she was picking up breakfast.

Then he got dressed and set up to the table. Soon she would be there.

Moments later the doorbell rang. Behind the door was Emily with a brown bag with the warm fresh croissants. He opened the door and greed Emily…"Bonjour Emily."

"Bonjour Pierre."

She came in and set the bag in the kitchen counter meanwhile Pierre turned the coffee machine in. They sat down they had breakfast. They made plans for Christmas and Pierre said would be a good idea for all to meet by Pierre's parents house in the country. Then Pierre kissed Emily. Then she left…"Au revoir Pierre."

Emily went down by the elevator and then out to the street. She went to see her parents at the hotel.

The few days ahead where wonderful for Emily. As soon as she got out from work she called her mother. They went shopping for Christmas gifts they went all over Paris.

Emily's father came along with the two of them for the help. By then Emily knew all good spots to shop around. They were enjoying the shopping and Emily's mother was very happy. Soon Emily would get married they returned back to Paris before their daughter's wedding.

Eighteen

Finally the night before Christmas arrived. Emily had packed a few of her essentials then she left. Pierre was just outside waiting for her. He drove her to the hotel. Emily went up to the hotel room.

She knocked at the door and her father opened the room.

"Good morning Emily."

"Good morning dad…mom. Are you two ready to leave?"

"Yes Emily." Her mother answered. They picked their bags and got ready to leave.

"Yes Emily. We can leave now."

They came down to the lobby. Emily's father hand in the room key. Then they all walked to the car where Pierre was waiting for them. They greed each other. "Good morning Madame…

Monsieur."

"Good morning Pierre."

They sat in the back of the car and a few minutes later drove away towards the countryside. It took Pierre one-hour drive meanwhile the time past fast.

When they knew it they had just arrived. They all got out of the car. Emily and Pierre walked in front while the older couple, just behind them.

Pierre knocked at the door they waited a few minutes. Then a woman with dark hair wearing a uniform opened the door. She was helping Pierre's mother with extra help for the few days during Pierre's mother with extra help for the few days during the Christmas season and especially with the extra guests.

"Bonjour Mademoiselle…Madame…Monsieurs."

They all walked in she had lead them to the living room. Then a few minutes Madame came to the living room. Then the housekeeper excused herself and went to the kitchen…"Pardon-moi."

"Bonjour Pierre…Emily entre."

"Bonjour ma mere."

"Bonjour Madame." Then Emily introduced her parents to Pierre's mother and father. Although Emily parents didn't spoke the French language Madame spoke just a little bit of English.

"Madame vous present ma mere pere."

"Enchante." "It is a pleasure to meet you Madame."

"How do you do."

Then Madame welcome them to their house…"Bievenue Madame…Monsieur."

Then they walked to the sitting room where her husband was reading the newspaper. Pierre greed his father and then at the same time introduced Emily's parents.

They sat down meanwhile Pierre's father prepared the drinks. Meanwhile Giselle the housekeeper took all the baggage from the trunk of the car. Then, she carried up to the rooms. Then came back and went to the kitchen to finish the food.

The day had seemed to pass quickly. Then it was time to dine meanwhile the guests went to change their clothing. After the dinner they all went to Church for the midnight mass. They drove into the town just a few kilometers from the house. But the service was in French it didn't matter.

It seemed that Pierre's parents were religious people. Everyone was happy soon. They would be a large family. When they came back from the Church service they all gathered around the Christmas tree. It was a small tree decorated with all the trimmings. Then they began to open their presents. Emily was anxious to open her present whichpresent, which it was a large box. She wondered what could be inside.

Meanwhile she saw Pierre opening his present from her. It was a simple man's ring with a square shape and it had diamonds. He opened his present and he was surprised. Emily was tearing the large package then she saw it was a very modern sewing machine.

She was happy. Then she could do her sewing faster and more precisely.

"Oh! Pierre it is wonderful merci." She hugged Pierre then just kissed him on his lips.

Pierre was delightful with his ring too, which it fit well. Pierre didn't know how Emily got the right measurement of his finger. She took one day without him noticed too much she used a tread to measure his finger. Everyone had opened their Christmas presents and they all were happy. Then they all sat in the reading room. Madame excused herself she went to the kitchen. She brought a large platter fill with small sandwichssandwiches olives crackers cheese.

Then Pierre went to help his mother as it was a tradition to eat after midnight mass.

Then they all ate and then it was time to say good night. Emily asked Madame if she needed any help. Madame thanked her for the offer. Giselle would be there early in the morning.

Then Madame said good night to Pierre and Emily. They both stayed a bit longer by themselves. They sat down in the floor closed to the fireplace it was still burning. They both held hands they looked at each other.

Pierre touched her hair then kissed her passionate. They both just kissed before going to their separate rooms.

The next day it was the Christmas day. Madame got up early to prepared the leg of lamb.

Meanwhile Giselle had prepared the table for breakfast then she made French toast for all the guests. After everything was done Giselle asked Madame if she could leave. She wished a happy Christmas day for everyone. Madame replied too…"Giselle avait un bon Noel."

"Merci Madame."

She left. Everyone was sleeping late. Later Pierre came down to wish his parents a happy Christmas.

"Bon fete de Noel." Pierre had said to his mother and father. When it came time for breakfast everyone sat down at the table. They all enjoyed each other company.

Then afterwards Pierre and Emily went for a walk in the woods. But Emily walked up to the room to get her coat. Meanwhile Pierre waited for the door he had his winter jacket.

"Viens avec moi Cherie."

"Oui Pierre."

The cloudy day didn't seemed to light up at all. It was a very chilly Christmas day. The countryside was so peaceful so different from the big city of Paris.

The air was so fresh which they needed once a while to get out from the city to the country. The wind began to blow really fast. Pierre got closer to Emily to warm her up. They walked for a little while then they stopped. They smiled their eyes lit up. They looked at each other. Then he said to her…"Emily je t'aime beaucoup." He kissed, and had their arms around each other.

He picked her up and then he found a spot in the ground. Emily lay on top of him. They touched each other. They made love just there; it didn't matter at all if it was cold. It made them feel better.

Then they both sat down for a few moments before going back to the house. They had been outside for along time they didn't notice it was late after all. They were walking back when they felt tiny snow flakess-nowflakes. It didn't amount too much it was the beginning to feel like Christmas like other ones that Emily remembered.

"Emily we should be going inside." Emily was surprised at Pierre for speaking English he usually spoke his native language.

"Oui Pierre. Nous allons maintenant."

They walked inside. Her mother told Pierre if he had forgotten the time…"Oui ma mere." It was time to serve the dinner. Madame needed there help…"Pardon moi Madame."

Pierre took his coat so did Emily. They both followed Madame into the kitchen, which, they help, to set the table. Quickly the table was set the food came to the table. Then moments later the Madame announced the dinner would be serve. Monsieur had gone to the wine cellar for the special wine.

After a long lavish dinner the coffee was taken to the next room. It was really dark and cold the snowflakes were much bigger. Then they all were gathered around they made a few plans for the wedding of Emily and Pierre.

Pierre wanted to be with Emily by he made an excused. He told them he was showing the town to Emily.

"Emily we are going for a ride."

"Oui Pierre."

They got ready and both walked out. Suddenly it became colder but it didn't matter. Pierre drove away from the country house to main road. A few kilometers down in the road there it was all the commerce. The small shops and the restaurants and cafes were all together in the main road.

He parked just in the street. They walked in sat down.

"Deux café au lait. S'il vous plait."

"Oui Monsieur."

Pierre reached Emily's hand. They looked at each other. There was sparkling in their eyes.

He bent his head and kissed her hand then he kissed her lips. They didn't mind if there was a crowd applauding them. They came apart soon the garcon brought their cafe au lait.

"Merci."

They talked for a little while then it was time to go back. When they got up people smiled at them.

Pierre waved.

It was half way to the house they stopped. Pierre drove towards the side of the road but in a safe place.

Pierre looked at Emily there they connected to each other. They kissed, they made love in there.

After a while they went back to the house. They walked in everyone were sitting in front of the fireplace.

"Come in in close to the fireplace."

"It is getting colder but it was a nice drive into to town."

Madame asked if everything was all right.

"Oui ma mere…Oui Madame."

They sat down close to each other and watched the logs burning. Then soon it was time to go to bed. The next day they will be departing to Paris.

Pierre said good night he went to his room and Emily quickly ran upstairs.

To say good night to him…"Bon nuit Pierre."

"Bon nuit Emily."

They embraced each other and kiss. Each one went to their rooms.

By the morning Emily was awake early. Then she got dressed and packed her belongings.

Afterwards she came down by then Pierre had came already. Then her parents follow her.

Then they all had a French continental breakfast. It was time to leave, they said their good byes.

They hoped to meet again soon.

Pierre drove away with Emily and her parents, back to Paris. It didn't take long for they to be in the city. He stopped at the hotel. Emily stayed with her parents she later in takes a taxi back to her place.

"Au adieu Pierre." She waved back to Pierre. Emily's parents were already up to their room.

Meanwhile Emily picked a newspaper to look at the ads. She pushed the up button and moments later she was knocking at the door.

"It is I Emily." Then her mother said for her to wait a minute. Her mother opened the door she was changing her clothing.

Emily wondered if they wanted to go out to some restaurant to eat or they would like to order room service.

They sat comfortable meanwhile Emily's father browsed through the brochures of different tours of the city.

Emily's mother was curious about Pierre she asked her some questions him and other matters.

But Emily was still looking at the ads. Emily needed to move from that place for something bigger.

There was a lot of work to be done in her drafting and making the clothing.

She was looking down in the last few ads of the column. She saw something that had appealed to her. The area was better then she wrote down the address.

Later they decided to have their lunch at the hotel. Then Emily's father went to the reception desk to book a tour.

Emily had just a few days before her parents left Paris to the North American Continental. By the time Emily left the hotel that day it was a very late. Then she took a taxi back to her roomy house.

Emily didn't have any classes until the second week of the New Year.

She would be very busy working at the boutique which everyone was trying to buy the elegant clothing for the New Year Eve parties although her parents were in Paris in New Year Eve, which everyone was trying to buy the elegant clothing for the New Year Eve parties although her parents were in Paris in New Year Eve, but Emily and Pierre wanted to spend the night together.

The day had arrives Emily up. He had planned to celebrate the new coming year in the special place. Then afterwards they went back to his apartment with champagne and strawberries. The midnight came and they kissed to celebration in private with me sound of soft music.

Then the day arrived for Emily's parents to leave. Emily took them to the airport until it was time to depart. They said their good bye Emily embraced her mother tight and her mother tight and her father.

Suddenly a tear fell down her mother's cheek she realized she was missing her daughter. But she would be all right so she would be back again to Paris.

Then moments later an announcer was announcing their flight for them to walk to the departure area. Emily waved to her parents until they disappear in sight. Emily took a taxi back to her work place. She had missed her classes but it was all right.

The next few days Emily went looking for the apartment that she had seen in the ad of the newspaper. Emily rang the doorbell waited a few minutes before someone answers back. A woman well dressed around the middle aged opened the door…"Oui. Mademoiselle." Emily answered very politely she was looking for the apartment which she saw the announcement in the newspaper.

"Oui Mademoiselle…Entre s'il vous plait."

"Merci."

The woman told her to follow her she walked up to the second floor. The staircase was wide and the steps were all in marble.

Then they walked around of a corridor. Madame opens the door they both went. Emily was very surprised how the apartment looked inside. It had high ceilings large windows and there was white door, which led to each room. The rooms were all furnished with simple classic furniture. The apartment was spacious and she liked it what she had seined a good place to move in.

The metro was close just a small distance away. Emily asked Madame how much she wanted for the month. The price was right she could afford it. Then she said…"Oui Madame…Je prend."

"Bien Mademoiselle."

She told Madame she couldn't move right away maybe in a week. Madame said it was all right. Emily wrote down the address of where she was working. The woman seemed to be happy from what she saw in her. Then she said for her to call before moving in.

When it was time to move from where she was. She told Helene mother and she was a bit sad.

She liked Emily she told her needs a bigger place. She understood the reason why even Helene was sad she would still see her at classes. Helene mothers wished her good luck.

The week passed quickly and Emily made a telephone call for the woman of the new apartment.

Then Madame told her it was all right to move in that Sunday.

Emily came down to see Helene mother. She embraced her and said good bye…"Au revoir Madame…

Merci Madame pour tout."

"Merci Mademoiselle…Au adieu."

Emily took a taxi to the new place. After a while she arrived and knocked at the door.

"Oh! Mademoiselle…le voila."

"Bonjour Madame."

"Entre s'il vous plait…Mademoiselle."

Emily sat down she tried to do some sketches for her portfolio. Afterwards she went out to eat but she didn't stayed to long. When she returned she went to bed and only took a few moments before she fell asleep.

The next day she got up earlier since the school was further away from her new place.

The following days she were very busy the days got bigger it did help in the sense. She had more time to do other basic things. She did some decorating in the apartment. She had everything in her apartment she decided to invite Pierre for dinner at the apartment.

She had everything in her apartment she decided to invite Pierre for dinner at the apartment.

When the time came. She had done something special.

She had an elegant dress in. She heard a knock at the door and then went to answer.

"Bonjour Pierre...entre."

"Merci Emily. Comment va vous?"

"Bien."

He smiled at her because they both knew they would have privacy at last without going to his place.

They embraced each other and then they kissed. Afterwards Emily said..."Mais mon, Pierre."

She had dinner ready and it was time for them to have dinner..."Bien Emily." They sat down to a candle light dinner.

After a marvelous dinner which Emily had done from scratch and she also had baked a simple cake. She brewed a pot of coffee while she waited she cut down two slices of cake.

The evening had to come to an end and Pierre had to leave. He had to be earlier at work next day. They kissed...they said good night..."Au revoir ma Cherie."

"Au revoir Pierre."

Emily tied everything up in the kitchen then she spent a little bit time doing sketches. She was preparing a different portfolio. She would be drafting the patterns and do the whole clothing from the beginning. She wanted to do some so she could be able to sell them at the Madame's boutique. Emily knew Madame liked her outfits.

Nineteen

The spring would be coming soon in a few weeks. She had to plan her wedding, as they will be marrying towards the end of spring and beginning of summer. Her classes would be ending soon.

A couple weeks later since Emily invited Pierre to the apartment. She had another fashion show to prepare and it would be the last one.

At the same time she had changed the drapes of the living room and bedroom. She bought a small television and asked the telephone, company to connect a telephone.

She had a more enjoyable area to live in weekends. She was putting down her ideas for her wedding dress.

One day she was sketching some of her designs.

She began sketching a long dress with a bodice tight with a round necklace. It was coming from the waist coming down with a slight train. The sleeves would be done in lace fabric so would be done in lace fabric so would the upper part of the dress. She went sketching until she was satisfied with design. It took her a little while she did it. That's what she wanted to be her wedding design. But with her other in her mind. She decided to find someone to do her wedding dress.

She spoke to the Madame maybe she would know someone. She wanted to wear her own creation.

Madame spoke of a woman whom she knew she could do her dress for a lower price a favor to Madame.

One afternoon she asked Madame if she could take the two hours off. She wanted to talked to the woman about the dress and Madame said…"Oui."

"Emily took her sketch to show. But she had done a second one. She described all the details and all other accessories she wanted to be put it in the dress.

When she arrived at the door of the address mention in her note-book. She saw a corridor, which at end of it it was portable closet. She walked to the waiting area there was fabric all over.

There were two mannequins with half, finished, out-fits with sewing and pins. The young woman said to Emily to wait a minute while she was calling Madame Marie.

Emily thanked the young woman…"Merci."

Moments later the Madame came from a room behind. She was well dressed but had a measuring tape around her neck. But still wasn't anyone she was expecting at all.

Madame had said to her she was expensive that meant she only did the clothing for a few clients.

"Bonjour Mademoiselle."

"Bonjour Madame."

"Oui…Je m'appelle Emily aussi je travaille dans une boutique."

"Ah! Oui."

Madame Marie recognized right away. She knew that her old friend had sender her. Madame presumed the young woman must be someone very special.

Madame was old fashion couturier and she had a very well clientele. She was an old friend of Emily employer. Madame got in touch once a while. Madame Marie was pleased to do Emily's wedding dress. Afterwards Emily showed her the sketch. Madame Marie liked it and saw that Emily had talent.

"Oui Mademoiselle Emily bien."

Madame Marie told Emily she would take care of everything. She would buy the special fabric. The only information needed was the wedding. But Emily couldn't tell her because they hadn't set the date yet. Emily will be in touched and soon she knew she would tell.

Madame told her she would call for her first fitting.

"Au revoir Madame Marie."

"Au revoir Emily." Then she left. She went back to work.

A few days passed since she had seen Madame Marie. She called Pierre and told him she had a couturier to do it. Pierre was happy and then they decided to meet next day.

They had their decision. They began to make their arrangements and the date was the last Saturday of the month of June.

Pierre spoke to his parents.

Finally springtime had arrived. Emily began to buy the new pieces of clothing for the season and others she done. The fashion show was a couple days away and she was ready.

Emily had also completed two outfits for the boutique and Madame was very impressed. Even the boutique customers asked about new clothing from the new designer.

Meanwhile Emily had two fittings of her wedding dress. It took only a couple days until the dress would be finished.

Emily was so happy. Pierre's parents arranged the appointment with the Church and the catering.

The wedding would be outside in the garden with a few friends and family.

Madame was so enthusiastic with Emily designs she wanted to help her to find a clothing manufacturer whom would use Emily's designs. Of course Madame would promote her designs in her boutique. After a few weeks looking around and getting all the information Madame found a manufacturer. Then both went to talked to person who was in charge. Emily showed her portfolio which she done recently.

Monsieur Larouche really liked and accepted her a designer. But she would starts working for them in the next season.

Emily was pleased at that moment. She embraced Madame with so much joy and gratitude. The executive was also pleased and wanted to give Emily's a chance.

Madame told Emily she could have the rest of the afternoon off. Emily called Pierre at his job he was busy. He couldn't get to the telephone. Then she left the message to call her back to the apartment.

She went to the market to get a few fresh fruits vegetables. She stopped at the butcher to buy a leg of lamb. She knew that Pierre loved roast lamb. Three hours later she received a telephone call from Pierre. She invited him for dinner at her apartment.

He said yes but it would be a bit later than the usually time. Emily set the table the dinner was ready. Then changed her clothing for something more sensuous. Meanwhile Emily waited for Pierre she sat down in the sofa writing a letter to her mother. She finished writing a letter to her mother and slip inside of an envelope. Suddenly she heard a knock at the door.

"Cet vous Pierre?" Emily asked out loud if was Pierre…"Oui Emily."

At that moment she opened the door…"Entre."

His left hand behind with a bouquet of flowers. He kissed her her lips then handed in her bouquet.

"Merci Pierre."

Pierre came in he could right away smell the dinner that she had been cooking. He was hungry. She lighted up a few candles the table he opened a bottle of red wine. Then both sat down at the table. Afterwards they sat in the sofa she told him the good news.

"Ma Cherie Emily."

"Merci Pierre. Maintenant tous va bien."

The time was approaching for their wedding. She wondered were they would be going to their honeymoon. Emily's apartment was perfect for them to live it was much bigger than his the area was also a good one.

Moments later Pierre gently put his arms around her and whisper in her ear…"Oui…oui."

He passionate kissed her he took in his arms and then lifted her and walked towards the bedroom. There they were so much heat and friction between the two of them.

They began touching each other. Pierre was pleasing her sexually and at the same time she did the same.

They stayed together for a few hours. For a moment both had forgotten their duties. Emily had her classes too go and Pierre had to go back to work. But never the less they had a wonderful evening.

Pierre then said good morning to her. He left. She had a few more hours of sleep.

The next day she was late for her classes. But it didn't matter and much thosedthose were the last days of classes. She had an already the grades and the fashion show had made her one of the best pupils of the year.

Finally the day came all the classes were all over. They had planned a party to celebrate the end of the school term. They all enjoyed themselves they hoped to be in touched with each other. They all left and all went their different ways.

Emily had her job at the boutique and the other job too.

But her boutique hours were cut down. She began her sketches for her new job. She had a few ideas for her new portfolio.

When she begin her work she told the management. She needed two week for her wedding and honeymoon. She would make it up later in. They agreed and she was relief.

Meanwhile everywhere she went she carried her sketchpad for all the any time she had to sketch her idea down. She was working in the fashion for the next season.

Her wedding dress was ready. On the follow weekend Pierre and Emily went to visit his parents in the countryside. They planned the two days confirming any wedding details. Everything was all ready and they waited for the wedding day. Emily's parents would be arriving soon in Paris they would stay at Pierre's parents, country home.

Afterwards they would go to the hotel.

Meanwhile Emily still had no idea about their honeymoon. She knew. Pierre had made some special plans he had spoke lightly about the matter.

The days seemed to pass quickly and soon the big day came closer. When Emily's parents arrived. She stayed all night working in her portfolio that she completed.

There was a moment of relief afterwards she had finished it before her wedding day.

Emily's parents would be arriving in the middle of the morning. Emily was very tired from working all night but she had to get ready. Although she had not sleep altogether two hours. The morning was very warm and she walked to the small balcony she took a big breath of fresh air. She felt awake then. The view from the balcony was fantastic even she could the Eiffel Towel. She smelled the fresh bread being earlier in the morning. There was the smell around Paris. She began to get a big appetite it must been from working all night.

She was by now used to live in a beautiful European city. She was considering Paris her home she had fallen in love with Paris and her lover. She had a full life her French got much better.

Emily must not forget why she was in Paris. The wonderful man she had fallen in love. She had a lot of expectations when she had arrived in Paris. It opened her eyes she had turned out to become a better person for. She was grateful for her parents for letting her to come to Paris for the first time.

Emily walked back inside of the apartment. She took a shower. After a while she felt better and got dressed. Then she left and went to Deux-Magots for le petit-dejeuner.

When she arrived there around nine o'clock. The place was full and she waited for a few minutes. Soon she saw an empty table she sat down. She orders the double toast and café au lait.

Then the garcon ate her warm toast with the French taste of butter. Then she made a signal to the garcon he approached the table. He politely asked her…"Oui Mademoiselle."

"Un autre café s'il vous plait."

"Bien Mademoiselle."

Emily relaxed before leaving to the airport. She knew she would have to wait for the arrival of the flight. They would have to wait for the arrival of the flight. They would stay overnight at the same hotel they had stayed before.

"Merci." She thanked the garcon for bringing the coffee. Later in she paid her breakfast.

Then she left. But she went to a public cabin to make a telephone call to Pierre.

Afterwards she waved for a taxi. When she got to the Galle airport which she had still time to spare. She checked for the flight from North Continental. It said in the monitor that would be arriving at fifteen minutes after eleven in the morning.

Emily bought a magazine and went to the lounge area for a little while.

She took a cool bottle of Perrier it was a warm morning. The airport was one of the busiest in Europe. Once a while she went to check the monitor for the arrival flight. Afterwards the flight had just arrived.

Emily waited until she saw her parents coming they both looked well dressed.

The porter, were carrying their baggage. Immediately they saw Emily they approached her and walked towards where she was. They embraced Emily at the same time…"How are you my dear?"

"I am fine thank you."

"Mom we better be moving along."

They talked outside for a little while bit…"We all missed you Emily."

"I have too."

"How is Pierre?"

"He is fine."

"We should be moving along don't you think so?"

"Yes father." They took to downtown Paris. Minutes later the taxi was at the front of the hotel.

They step out of the taxi the driver took the baggage…"Merci Mademoiselle."

Her father checked in. Moments later they were in their room it had a greater view.

"Merci Mademoiselle." The porter thanked Emily she tipped.

They all sat down Emily began the conversation with her parents.

"Father…how are the business?"

"Emily everything is well. I have someone in charge one younger executive. This way I your mother can travel all around the world. It is about time."

"That is a good father. You need a break from all those hard years of working."

"Emily how are you adapting to Paris?" Her mother was asking her she wondered if she missed home.

"I doing well and everything are well better than I had expected. Now I am working direct into a clothing manufacturer. I have completed a whole season.

"I am proud of you Emily." Her mamma approached closer to her…"Yes Emily. We are proud of you and we wished a happy marriage too."

"Thank you father…mother. I thank you for your support."

They all were very tired. But they didn't wanted to rest otherwise they would have difficulty sleeping later.

They were having jet leg. Even Emily was terrible tired she had to watch out too.

Emily asked if they wanted something to eat. Perhaps the room services would be appropriate.

Since they all were very tired to go anywhere.

"Emily…it is a good idea. We will eat something light."

Meanwhile Emily looked at the brochures they had in the table. She looked at the one with the room service.

She looked through and chose something for all and for her too. Her mother was unpacking just a few pieces of clothing. They would be leaving the next day. But they would come back after the wedding. The reservations had been made already. They would be spending a few days in the country-side. It was a good time for them to relax and enjoyed the company of the new family to be.

Emily looked and with confidence chose something and called room services. In half an hour knocked at the door. Emily answered she opened the door…"Merci."

Emily's father signed in. But she tipped the garcon…

"Merci Mademoiselle."

He left. They began to eat…"This looks all right Emily." Her father thanked her daughter.

Afterwards Emily left. She would be in touch with them.

She took the metro to her nearest stop to the apartment.

She picked her black portfolio and left, right way her destination. She went to see the management of her new work. She didn't have an appointment but it was important. She had waited because the person was busy he would see her. After waiting a long while the secretary said to her she could go in.

Politely she spoke to Monsieur Elliot.

"Bonjour Mademoiselle Emily."

"Voici ma dossier Monsieur."

"Bien Emily merci."

"C' estest. tous maintenat Mademoiselle."

Then she left his office. She was glad. Monsieur Elliot would get in touch with her telephone.

He would call her next day after checking in her designs. But she had still a few days before her wedding.

She went straight to the boutique. Although she was feeling a bit exhausted to go to work.

Maybe she could get out earlier if the shop was not to crowd. When she arrived at the boutique Madame was writing something in her stationary there were none of the customers.

"Bonjour Emily."

"Bonjour Madame."

"Emily est-ce que vous etes fatigue?"

"Oui je suis un peau."

Madame told her to straighten up the clothing racks and shelves. Since Madame right way noticed Emily was herself. She told her if there were no customers could leave earlier. She thanked Madame for her suggestions. She done the things she was supposed to and at the same time she done her widow display.

The afternoon was quiet slower than usual. Madame told Emily she could leave.

So she did.

By the time she reached the apartment she couldn't take another step. Although her parents were in town she called them. She wanted to know she call them. She wants to know how they were. She would be in touch next day.

Emily puts the receiver down Pierre calls. He wanted to know if her parents had arrived.

When would he be picking, them up which he will be taking to his parents she told him after breakfast.

Afterwards she went straight to bed. She was exhausted for having almost no sleep the night before. Moments later she was in a deep sleep.

Meanwhile her parents had rested in that afternoon. They were very much rested. They came down to the lobby and then afterwards they walked to the restaurant. They knew already the hotel.

Emily felt better after a couple hours of sleep. She was awake by the sounds of a hard knock at her door. She came running, towards the door to seewhatsee what person it was making all the knocking. She opened the door there he was holding a bouquet of fresh flowers. She was surprised to see Pierre he stood there. Immediately Emily apologized for taking so long she was asleep.

"Bonsoir Emily. Comment va vous?"

"Bonsoir Pierre. Je suis bien maintenat. Entre s'il vous plait."

Pierre walked inside they sat in the sofa. Since she slept for along time when she noticed it was time for dinner. She asked him if he had dinner yet.

"Pierre avez-vous dine?"

"Non Emily. C'est la raison que je suis ici."

Pierre had come to ask Emily out for dinner.

"Oui Pierre nous allons."

Emily quickly went to change her clothing. She came out from her bedroom looking very beautiful. She went to the kitchen for a minute to set the flowers in a long vase.

Ten minutes later they left the apartment. Pierre had parked the car in the another side street close by.

Then he drove towards the restaurant. But he had not made any reservations. Therefore there was no table. Meanwhile they waited they had an aperitif.

"Dubonnet deux s'il vous plait."

"Bien Monsieur."

It was a very busy hour it didn't takes for them to sit. The maitre d' showed the their table.

"Merci."

They dine they talked for a little. Although there were just a few clues, which Pierre told Emily she needed for their honeymoon. She needed evening, wear and casual clothing. But,

Pierre didn't say other word. The rest of the evening was calm. Then he suggested after the dinner they could for a stroll in the avenue of Champs-Elysees. Afterwards they will have an espresso in the side walk-sidewalk café.

"Oui Pierre maintenat je n'est suis pas fatigue." "Bien nous allons maintenant."

He drove towards the famous avenue he parked close by in one of the side streets. They walked up the street holding hands. They walked a little bit then. It was time for them to seat down for an espresso and a cappuccino.

The evening was still beautiful suddenly there was a wind. Emily felt great she was so much in love with Pierre. Also she was enchanted with Paris. The city was full of romance anywhere in the city.

"Oui Monsieur…Mademoiselle."

"An espresso une cappuccino s'il vous plait."

"Oui Monsieur."

The sidewalks were full of crowds they were passing by close the cafes. Pierre held Emily's hands they were a few days before they got married.

Emily was now a designer. She had completed second year course she enjoyed all the way.

"Merci." Pierre thanked the garcon when he brought the espresso and the cappuccino.

The sidewalks were full of crowds they passing by the cafes. Pierre held Emily's hand they were enjoying their last bachelor days.

Emily was now a designer. She had completed the second year course.

"Merci." Pierre thanked the garcon.

They spoke for a little while until her father had finished at the reception desk and then he walked to the sofa.

"Are you too ready to go for breakfast."

"Yes father." Emily smiled then got up. Mother got up they all walked towards the restaurant. They had breakfast meanwhile they talked to each other.

Emily was enjoyed the company of her parents soon she would be married and will change her life.

Probably once a while, her parents would visit her and her husband in Paris. They had an excuse to come more often.

They knew that her daughter was very happy.

When they came from the restaurant. Pierre was waiting in the lobby. Emily walked up to Pierre and her parents follow her. She kissed him then her parents greeted him. They made a few plans before leaving. But Emily had to work a few more days before her wedding. They were taking them. They went up to their room to pick up her luggage.

Twenty

Minutes later the older couple came down. Then they said good bye-good-bye to Emily. They got into Pierre's car. He drove away he waved to Emily. On the reception desk of the hotel she dials to the operator to place an outside call. Minutes, later Emily was in the telephone speaking to Madame. Then she walked out and walled to the nearest metro. Half an hour later she stepped inside of the boutique.

"Bonjour Madame."

"Bonjour Mademoiselle Emily."

Emily had a lot of work to do. She needed to change the window display but she looked into the shelves to pick the right clothing and its accessories. She needed more time to do it. She wanted to leave the boutique with a nice display. Meanwhile Madame was looking for someone for part-time to be able to replace Emily while she was away.

Madame had a few applications she was still looking for more. She would help Madame with the interview.

When it came the time for lunch she had almost done the window she had a little bit of time. She walked a few times outside to see if she liked it what she did.

Then left smiling she walked a little bit and took the metro. She decided to go some wheresomewhere different. She went to the Galleries Lafayettes and she would stay longer.

At the main floor she needed a few creams and eau toilette and other essentials. She looked in her list and she also needed new underwear. She wanted to buy something elegant.

Emily went through the lingerie area she looked through the racks of all types of lace different colors and sets of nightgowns and robes matching. She was looking in one of the particular rack when she discovered a beautiful set with a V-neck. All embroidered around the neckline and the bodice. The fabric was organza with in a cream color. She picked her size and then asked to go try it in.

She had choice the right size everything fit well. But she also needed a shorter set.

She picked a few more pieces. Afterwards she went looking to other floors. There she picked a nice weekend bag and a matching luggage. Then she went for lunch near by. She was walking outside she

Sees tourists going by with their hanging cameras they could be spotted right away. She remembers being one of them.

When she returned to the boutique there were a few customers. Then Madame had an interview with young woman later in that afternoon.

Time passed quickly then the interview of a young woman happen Emily assisted Madame. She listened to Madame interviewing the young girl. Her name was Simone. Then Madame spoke afterwards to Emily.

"Oui Simone…Je pense qu'elle avait quelque chose comment vous ma cherie Emily."

"Oui Madame c'etait une bonne idee."

Emily hoped Simone would help Madame look and looked after the boutique. It won't be the same her but she to do.

"Bien Emily."

After closing the boutique Emily stayed for a little longer she organized all the merchandise.

Meanwhile they spoke about Emily's wedding. Madame wondered if she was nervous about it. Madame notices Emily being so quiet but Madame knew also she had a lot in her mind.

Then it was time for them to leave…"Bonsoir Madame."

"Bonsoir ma Cher Emily."

Afterwards Emily went straight to her apartment. By the time she arrives. She made something light to eat. Then she tried to call Pierre. But she couldn't reach him.

Moments later she was ready to go to sleep. She had fallen asleep. There she was dreaming already when she was awake by a sound of the telephone.

She turned the lights in in her night table and got up and answered.

It was Pierre in other side of the line. Pierre recognized right that Emily voice sounded strange.

He asked he if she was all right. She answer she had been asleep for a while.

Pierre apologizes for awaking her up. Then he put her mind in ease saying her parents were all right. Then they spoke for a little while then they said their good nights.

"Bien Emily. C'est tout. Bon nuit."

"Bon nuit Pierre."

Then Emily walked back to the bedroom and went back to sleep. She wondered how they would get along with her future in-laws somehow the night hours passed quickly into the hours of morning. Emily soon was awake by the sunlight through the light white drapes. She felt a bit sleepy. But she had to get up. She finished dressing. When the telephone rang a few times then she answered. "Oui."

"Mademoiselle Emily?"…A male voice asked wondered if he had the right number.

"Ici c'est Monsieur Elliot."

"Oui Monsieur." Emily wonders what Monsieur wanted. Then he told her he wanted to see her…"Oui."

Then she left. But she had some breakfast before getting to Monsieur Elliot office.

Meanwhile she had a fast breakfast in one of her favorite places. Then it was time to go see Monsieur Elliot. By the time she got there she waited until her secretary said she could go in.

"Bonjour Mademoiselle Emily."

"Bonjour Monsieur."

He sat down in front of his desk he had her portfolio opened. He began to look at her designs.

"Mademoiselle…Je veux voir ici." He didn't finish the whole sentence.

Then he told her the designs she had drawn were very good. He would begin the production of those designs. He was very pleased with her. She thanked him for giving her a chance. Monsieur Elliot wished her best.

"Bon chance Mademoiselle."

"Au revoir Monsieur."

"Au revoir Mademoiselle."

She left.

Later in she arrived at the boutique. Madame was glad she arrived. She was swamp with customers. The new young woman Simone would be starting in the afternoon. It was closed for the lunch Pierre showed up.

She was surprise of him being there.

"Bonjour Emily."

"Bonjour Pierre. Comment ca va vous?"

"C'est une surpris."

Pierre asked her if she was free for lunch. He would like to go out for lunch with her. Some place different…"Oui mais…" She would have to ask Madame if she could stay a little longer.

"Oui Mademoiselle."

Emily finished attending her last customer. Then she went to get ready…"Bien au revoir Madame."

"Au revoir Mademoiselle…Monsieur."

"Au revoir Madame."

The two of them left holding hands they walked up to the car. Pierre had something special in his mind. It was in a beautiful summer day. These days were one of the lasts days a bachelor couple.

Pierre took her to the Eiffel Towel. Emily was delightful for him choosing that restaurant.

The wine waiter brought a bottle of French champagne. Afterwards they toasted then he took a small package from his pocket. He took it and put it in the table.

"Oh Pierre je t'aime."

Pierre held her hands and smiled at her. She opened the small package there it was a beautiful gold necklace and a heart. Emily liked it. Then she said…"Merci Pierre."

Emily was astonished because she wasn't expecting any presents from him. They had their desserts and the coffee. Then left Eiffel Tower. Then he took her back to the boutique. It was already two thirty in the afternoon. But Madame didn't mind at all. She knew she would make it up. When she arrived, Simone was already.

"Bonjour Simone." Emily greed her. Then Pierre left.

"Au revoir Emily."

"Au revoir Pierre."

Simone was eager to learn from Emily. The whole afternoon Simone watched Emily how she took care of the clients and the little details.

Then it was time to close the boutique. Madame wanted to speak to Emily. She was about to work one more day before she left to her future in-laws.

Emily afterwards went shopping she still had time to do a little bit of shopping. There were still some shops opened. When she arrived at her apartment she began packing. She ate something in the way to her apartment.

She began to look for the clothing that she would need for her honeymoon. She had her wedding dress in a long bag. So no one could see it specially Pierre. She had all her accessories for her wedding dress.

She had bought a pair of elegant shoes and the clear panty hose for her to wear with the shoes. She checks her beauty case to see if she had missed anything. She finished packing and was ready for the next day when Pierre would pick her up late afternoon.

She wasn't sure the time. She got ready to go to sleep she needed a good one.

The next day she got up and went for breakfast the to the boutique. All she left everything by the sofa.

She entered the boutique smiling.

"Bonjour Madame."

"Bonjour Emily. Vous etait content aujourd'hui."

"Oui Madame."

"Je savais pourquoi."

"Oui Madame."

"Bonjour Simone."

"Bonjour Mademoiselle."

Simone was there earlier than Emily. She had today, to look how Emily done and looked after the customers. Emily went in helping Madame. The boutique customers said their good bye to Emily and wished her the best. They were used to Emily she helped them the best she knew how.

Then it was time to leave. She said au revoir to Madame and Simone. Then went straight to her apartment.

She checked the apartment and watered her plants. Then changed something casual. Then changed something casual. Then tied everything up. She was ready to leave. She waited for Pierre.

Emily sat down in the sofa she browsed through the magazine. Then moments later there was a knock at the door.

She came back to the present then opened the door.

"Bonjour Pierre…entre s'il vous plait."

"Bonjour Emily…vous va bien?"

"Je suis tres Pierre."

Pierre looked down and saw Emily's baggage ready to be picked up. Then he began to pick and carry downstairs to the car…"Emily je peux."

"Oui."

Pierre took all her baggage. Then he would come back.

Minutes, later Pierre was back again. Meanwhile Emily pulled the curtains. Then she was ready to leave. She picked the long bag and carried with her then locked the door.

Moments later they were inside of the car. Pierre drove away. They would have dinner with Pierre's parents and Emily's too. They were very quiet all the way.

Pierre would be sleeping over a friend house. So he wouldn't Emily in the wedding day.

They would see each other in the Church. They arrived. Emily was the first one to walk up to the door.

Giselle opened the door…"Bon soir Mademoiselle."

"Bon soir Giselle."

Emily walked in moments later Madame came to greed her. She was in the kitchen with Emily's mother. Pierre's were some wheresome-where else.

Emily's mother heard a voice she came out of the kitchen. She embraced her daughter.

"How are you Emily."

"Mamma…I am feeling all right but a bit nervous. How is father?"

"He is well and enjoying himself. Where is Pierre."

"He is well and enjoying himself. Where is Pierre."

"He is bringing all the baggage inside."

Then Madame spoke to her guests she said dinner would be served in half an hour. Madame

Saw Pierre with his hands full and asked Giselle to help Pierre.

Giselle took Emily's baggage to her room. Then she quickly went up to her room for that night to leave her special long bag.

Minutes later everyone was having dinner. After dinner Giselle brought their coffee then she tied it the kitchen then left.

Everyone was more relaxed they stayed for a little while. Then it was time to go to bed.

They said their good nights. Then Pierre left to his friend house to stay the night.

The last day came at last-a very special Saturday. The sun was bright then it was time to get up. Emily's mother went into her room and tried to awake her daughter up. She smiled at Emily and greed her.

"Good morning honey. It is time to get up this is your special day."

"Emily do you need any help now?"

"Mother…later in."

Her mother left. Emily stood still in bed. Some how there was a slightly case of nervous. Although she didn't wanted to tell her mother. She closed her eyes for a few more minutes. But those few minutes turned out to be an hour.

When she was awake again by a knock at her door…

"Oui entre."

"Bonjour Mademoiselle. Le voila votre petit-dejeuner."

"Merci Giselle."

She left a tray with warm croissants and some fresh squeezed juice and coffee. She knew that was Madame who had sent the tray. After all was a special day for Emily she was been pamper well.

She began eating and then she got ready.

She does her face and then her hair. She had her white satin robe in and she was about to dress her long white dress. Suddenly there was a knock at her door…"Entre"

There it was Madame with a beautiful bouquet of white and pink, roses…"Bonjour Emily. Vous-etes bien?"

"Bonjour Madame. Je suis bien merci."

Madame told her everyone were all ready. The photographer was ready to begin to take the photos.

The caterers were arranging everything outside in the garden. Emily asked Madame to ask her mother to come up to see her…"Bien Emily"

"Mamma…I need you to help me to get dress."

Emily took her dress from the garment bag. Slowly began to show it to her mother. She was astonished from what she had seeing. She couldn't believe how beautiful the dress was and after all she had design her own dress.

Emily had done a lot of sketches until she had found the right one she like it.

"Emily…I am proud of you honey. This is beautiful design of your wedding dress."

"Thank you mamma. It took a lot of sketches. But it was this one I liked the most."

Emily slipped the dress in and her mother to buttoned the tiny satin buttons in the back.

She made a beautiful bride. Then her mother embraced her daughter she kissed her in both cheeks.

…"Mother this day is very special for me knowing you and dad are here for my wedding…Mother I love Pierre very much."

"I know dear. We wished you the best for you too."

Then her mother helped Emily to put the veil in which it was a bit difficult to do it alone.

She was ready and with a smile in her face. Madame came in and smiled at her. She asked

Her if she could tell the photographer to begin to take the photos.

"Oui Madame. Je suis pretes."

"Bien."

Emily's embraced her daughter once more and she thanked her.

"Thank you mamma for being here."

Moments later a strong hand was knowing at her room…"Oui entre." "Merci Mademoiselle."

The photographer began snapping his camera which in an hour he had finished taking all the photos. Emily was ready to go to the Church.

The chauffeur then took Emily and her father to the Church. The other guests and the rest of family were following them.

The church was up in the narrow street. It was beautiful inside they had decorated with lost of flowers. Inside of the Church the guests had arrived.

There were already the family and a few friends. Emily slowly got out from the car she tried not to step in her long veil. She held onto to her father's arm.

Slowly she began walking the few steps to the inside of the church. She smiles, as she carried the white and pink roses in her hand. Meanwhile the French photographer was taking the photos.

Finally there she stood by Pierre's side. They held hands they stood still. Then the priest began the wedding ceremony. It came the time to say yes.

There was silence. Then Pierre said…"Oui je accepte Emily."

They both had their wedding bands the priest blessed them. Afterwards Pierre slowly lifted her veil from her face. Then he saw how beautiful she looked at that moment. He came closer to her kissed her and didn't matter who was around them that was their special moment. He whisper in her ear.

"Mon amour je t'aime."

Emily smiled at him…"Oui mon cherie Pierre. J'aime aussi."

Twenty-one

The young married couple walked down in the aisle. The car was waiting for them they stepped.

They were smiling and there was happiness in their eyes. Pierre got closer to Emily he gentle kissed her in the lips. Then they embraced they were happy.

The driver took back to the house. There were already some guests and the others would follow the bride and groom.

Everything was ready for the reception. The caterers were doing a good job.

A few kilometers from the house Pierre kissed Emily again. They would have less time for themselves for a little while.

Minutes later the chauffeur stop in front of the house and opened the door. Emily stepped out from the car then Pierre followed her.

Giselle come walking towards the couple and congratulated them.

Moments later their both parents arrived at the house.

Later the young couple walked to the garden where the guests were. They began to mingle with their guests.

Two hours later it was time to cut the wedding cake and toasted each other with champagne.

Afterwards Emily and Pierre went inside.

Emily changed into her linen pantsuit and her silky shirt and matching jacket.

Pierre also changed his formal wear into hiss casual clothes. Emily let her long hair down and retouched her lips with lipstick. Then they were both ready to come down.

They walked outside in the garden they thanked guests and said au adieu.

Emily approached her parents and embraced her mother and father.

"Thank you mamma for being here."

"We glad to be here. We will be in the morning for Paris where we will stay a few more days before we leave. Emily will be happy honey. We will be in touch later in."

Her father spoke and embraced her.

"Father…we will be in touch."

At that moment Pierre went to see Emily. He also thanked her parents. Before they left Pierre and Emily went to say their good bye to Pierre's parents. They embraced and they wished them a nice honeymoon.

They came inside the house to get their baggage and then it was time to leave.

"Nous allons Emily."

"Oui Pierre."

The couple got in the car Pierre drove away. After being in the road for a little while Pierre asked Emily to look in the glove department of the car. She was really curious about it. There was the answer where they were going in their honeymoon.

Pierre had a map of France that showed a few places marked with red pen. He had chosen the Mediterranean coast. Emily got very excited she looked to the places in the map…Marseille Niece Monte Carlo Cannes…But it were a long way so many kilometers, they would stop in various inns and small places.

Pierre had marked the route E1

Emily was happy Pierre once a while touched Emily while he was driving. It was a wonderful feeling. Pierre drove for a little while he stopped at a country side inn.

He walked in the reception desk. The middle age man was reading his newspaper while waiting for the tourists passing by.

Pierre said…Bon nuit. Monsieur. Je veux une chambre pour la nuit s'il vous plait."

Monsieur looked up and said…"Oui Monsieur. Le voila votre cle."

"Merci Monsieur." Pierre signed in the register book. Pierre took they key and went to the car.

"Emily…viens mon amour."

Pierre opened the door Emily walked in. Then he closed the door. They only unpacked the essentials for the night because in the next morning they would be leaving.

Emily excused herself she went inside of the small bathroom. Quickly she undressed and slipped the beautiful embroidery night-gown. She took off her make-up brushed her teeth and dipped a little bit of her favorite French perfume.

Meanwhile Pierre was ready and he only needed a few minutes in the bathroom. He turned the lights off.

Afterwards Emily came into the room. There was silence they didn't spoke to each other.

Emily smiled at Pierre.

"Une minute ma cherie."

Pierre had something in his hand and stepped into the bathroom. Meanwhile Emily tried the mattress, which it was a bit hard. But that had to do for the evening. She took some outfit for the next day. She looked herself in the mirror although there was still a small soft light.

Moments, later Pierre came out. They were their first night as, husband and wife. It wasn't a very romantic room they were travelling for a while. They would have better places to sleep in later in.

Pierre took Emily in his arms kissed her with so much passion. They forgot where they were in that small and uncomfortable.

He gently lay her in bed they kissed and began making love to each other. They caressed each other in way they hadn't done before.

He tried to be gentle with her and she tried to pleasure him too.

Moments, later they were apart for a few minutes. They reflected how wonderful they were being to each other.

Pierre also asked Emily if she wanted something to drink or eat. Since they had ate earlier than usual.

"Yes Pierre it would be nice something to drink maybe something simple to eat too."

Pierre looked to see if there was any telephone in the room. But he didn't see anyone.

He put in his pants and a shirt and told Emily he would go to check in the reception desk.

Pierre didn't see no one there was a bell to ring for any assistance. The older man came out Pierre apologizes for waking him up. The Monsieur said it was quiet all right. He asked if there was a possibility to have something to eat and drink. The Monsieur said yes. He would be asking his wife for her to prepare something in the kitchen.

A half an hour Monsieur came with a tray full of little appetizers and two glasses with a bottle of champagne.

Pierre knocked at the door and said…"C'est moi Pierre."

"Un moment Pierre."

Emily opened the door she saw him with a tray. He lay the tray in the table and he opened the chill bottle and poured into the glasses. They made a toast to each other.

"Pour nous."

"Bien…pour nous." They touched each other glass. It was good they ate pieces of cut cheese and bread. There were a few pieces of fruit and some pastries.

They were both hungry to eat everything there was in the tray. Pierre poured a little bit more of champagne into the glasses.

"Emily ma Cherie maintenant tu va bien?"

"Oui je suis bien." "I was bit hungry too Emily. I guess you were too."

"Yes Pierre. We didn't eat much at the reception."

They finished all the champagne and then they went back to bed. In the morning they would be moving along. Meanwhile they needed to rest they slept under the plain white sheets. They kissed and made love until they fell asleep.

They slept late they packed there clothing and got dressed casual. Before they left the country inn they asked the innkeeper if there were some place closed by which they could have breakfast.

The innkeeper told them they could have breakfast. They did any food preparation for the guests that requested it. Since most of the times they prefer to have some wheresomewhere else.

Pierre and Emily walked through the corridor at the end there was a small dining room but with huge windows looking to outside.

Meanwhile they both chose something simple. Madame prepared a typical French breakfast for the tow of them. Twenty minutes later Madame brought a tray and served them. Everything smelled good they tasted. They both liked.

Afterwards Pierre paid for the room and their food. The innkeeper and Madame wished them good luck in their marriage and the trip.

"Bon chance."

"Merci."

"Au adieu."

Two days later they arrived at Marseilles. They walked to the tourist information for booklets about the Cote d'Azur. Emily really was surprise she heard good things about the famous part of France.

They sat down for a while they browsed through the information special places to eat and to visit. They were various places they wanted visited Cannes Niece and Monaco.

They had marked down the casino of Monaco but it was stilled a while.

They enjoyed each and every day and every night was spent in a different place. They made passionate love every chance they had. At the end of each day they were very exhausted. They walked and they also wanted to spend time on the beach in various places.

Three weeks later all the excitement of the holidays it came to an end. They it was time to go back. They returned to Paris that it took less time. They only stopped when it was necessary.

After so many kilometers driving, Pierre was so exhausted. Emily was fine she had rested well. Pierre moved to Emily's apartment that was their place.

The next few days Emily tried to arrange and decorate the apartment differently.

Pierre went back to his job while she was busy at her work. Although, she had brought, a lot times her work back home. She had a lot of designing to be done for along while.

Emily was very happy with her marriage.

Emily has been working for the manufacturer for a year. The management was very satisfied with her designs and her ideas that she had brought with her.

Emily did a lot of thinking and afterwards she consulting with her husband. She realizes that it isn't enough. She wanted to move on.

Then springtime arrived. As young married couple they both were enjoying their new life.

Emily was very confident with herself decided to open her own small boutique with her own designs.

Finally the day arrived she opened her own boutique officially.

She invited her special friends whom helped her to be where she was.

Even her friend from her school days and the first most important person was Madame.

She received a fax from her parents congratulating her.

Pierre was very proud of her and toasted her to her future success. He had always supported her.

She thanked her friends from being there…Merci mes amis. Bienvenue a boutique…

…Les dessins de Emily's.

THE END

www.ingramcontent.com/pod-product-compliance
Lightning Source LLC
Chambersburg PA
CBHW022202050726
47590CB00002B/612